"It's hard for me to keep business separate from other things in this situation."

"Other things?" She lifted a brow.

Hell, he'd gone and said something he probably shouldn't have. And yet, if he couldn't be honest with her, then she had no reason to reciprocate. "I like you, Yvette. I feel protective toward you more than because it's my job."

Her nervous smile was too brief. "I like you, too, Jason Cash. I wish we could have met under different circumstances."

"Doesn't mean things can't go how we want them to."

"No, it doesn't." Now the smile returned, more confident.

STORM
WARNING

USA TODAY Bestselling Author
MICHELE HAUF

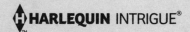

Recycling programs
for this product may
not exist in your area.

ISBN-13: 978-1-335-64072-7

Storm Warning

Copyright © 2019 by Michele Hauf

www.Harlequin.com

Printed in U.S.A.

Michele Hauf is a *USA TODAY* bestselling author who has been writing romance, action-adventure and fantasy stories for more than twenty years. France, musketeers, vampires and faeries usually feature in her stories. And if Michele followed the adage "write what you know," all her stories would have snow in them. Fortunately, she steps beyond her comfort zone and writes about countries and creatures she has never seen. Find her on Facebook, Twitter and at michelehauf.com.

Books by Michele Hauf

Harlequin Intrigue

Storm Warning

Harlequin Nocturne

The Witch's Quest
The Witch and the Werewolf
An American Witch in Paris
The Billionaire Werewolf's Princess
Tempting the Dark
This Strange Witchery
Ghost Wolf
Moonlight and Diamonds
The Vampire's Fall
Enchanted by the Wolf

In the Company of Vampires

Beautiful Danger
The Vampire Hunter
Beyond the Moon

Visit the Author Profile page at Harlequin.com.

CAST OF CHARACTERS

Jason Cash—Forced out of the CIA after a failed mission, and now a small-town police chief, Jason lands the case of a lifetime—and a chance for redemption—when a foreign spy tests his need to protect and serve. Is she or isn't she innocent?

Yvette LaSalle—An Interpol agent with a photographic memory who doesn't know what evidence she carries in her head is alone in a foreign country with only a sexy police chief to protect her from the forces who want her dead.

Jacques Patron—Assistant Director of Interpol who is protecting Yvette from what she knows. Or is he?

Herve Charley/James Smith—He's in Frost Falls on a mission that doesn't seem to go quite as planned.

Marjorie Thorson—Secretary/dispatcher/former nurse who is a second mom to Jason and would love to see him find the perfect woman.

Chapter One

Jason Cash squeezed the throttle on the snowmobile he handled as if a professional racer. The
five-hundred-pound sled took to the air for six
bliss-filled seconds. Snow sprays kissed Jason's
cheeks. Sun glinted in th⸺ ⸺ ⸺rystals.
The m⸺chine landed ⸺ ⸺ ⸺gliding
⸺ the powder. And
⸺n it involved grip- ⸺e grin
⸺d the
⸺ed with neon-green ⸺sota
⸺e tugged down the
⸺nose and mouth to
⸺eed, a coun-
⸺ears. His morning ride
through the pristine birch forest that cupped
the town on the north side had been interrupted
by a call from his secretary/dispatcher through
that same feed. He couldn't complain about the
missed winter thrills when a much-needed mystery waited ahead.

Maneuvering the snowmobile through a choppy
field with shifts of his weight, he steered toward
a roadside ditch, above which were parked the

city patrol car and a white SUV he recognized as a county vehicle. Sighting a thick undisturbed wedge of snow that had drifted from the gravel road to form an inviting ridge, Jason aimed for the sparkling payload, accelerated and pierced the ridge. An exhilarated shout spilled free.

Gunning the engine, he traveled the last fifty feet, then braked and spun out the back of the machine in a spectacular snow cloud that swirled about him. He parked and turned off the machine.

Flipping up the visor and peeling off his helmet, he glanced to the woman and young man who stood twenty yards away staring at him. At least one jaw dropped open in awe.

A cocky wink was necessary. Jason would never miss a chance to stir up the ▮▮▮▮ every day was a good day whe▮▮▮ ping it and ripping it.

Setting his helmet emblazon▮▮ fire on the snowmobile seat, ▮▮ thermal face mask from his ▮▮▮ hook under his chin. The thermostat read a nippy ten degrees. Already ice crystals formed on the sweat that had collected near his eyebrows. He did love the brisk, clean air.

It wasn't so brutally cold today as it had been last week when temps had dipped below zero. But the warm-up forecast a blizzard within forty-eight hours. He looked forward to snowmobiling through the initial onset, but once the storm hit full force, he'd hole up and wait for the pristine powder that would blanket the perimeter of the Boundary Waters Canoe Area Wilderness, where he liked to blaze his own trails.

Clapping his gloved hands together, he strode over to his crack team of homicide investigators. Well, today they earned that title. It was rare Frost Falls got such interesting work. Rare? The correct term was *nonexistent*. Jason was pleased to have something more challenging on his docket than arresting Ole Svendson after a good drunk had compelled him to strip to his birthday suit and wander down Main Street. A man shouldn't have to see such things. And so frequently.

He almost hated to share the case with the Bureau of Criminal Apprehension, but Marjorie had already put in a call to them. Someone from the BCA would arrive soon. Standard procedure when a homicide occurred within city limits.

"Cash." Alex Larson, who had just graduated from the police academy and headed north from the Twin Cities to find work, with hopes of eventually getting placed on search and rescue, nodded as Jason walked nearer. The tall, gangly man was twenty-four and had an eye for safety and a curiosity for all things female. Unfortunately, most of the women in Frost Falls were over forty. Not many of the younger ones stuck around after high school. Smart move in a dying town. The Red Band iron mine had closed four years ago.

That closure had sent the migrant workers—and far too many locals—packing in search of a reliable paycheck.

Alex was the only officer Jason needed in the little town of Frost Falls, population 627.

Though, from the looks of things, the population was now 626.

A middle-aged woman, wearing a black goose-down coat that fell to her knees and bright red cap, scarf and mittens, stood beside Alex. Elaine Hester was a forensic pathologist with the St. Louis County medical examiner's office. She traveled the seven-hundred-square-mile area so often she joked about selling her property in Duluth and getting herself an RV. She gestured toward the snowy ditch that yet sported the dried brown heads of fall's bushy cattails. The forthcoming blizzard would clip that punky crop down to nothing.

"What have you got, Elaine?" Jason asked, even though his dispatcher, Marjorie, had already told him about the body.

Jason led the team toward the ditch and saw the sprawled female body dressed in jeans and a sweater—no coat, gloves or hat—long black hair, lying facedown. The snow might have initially melted due to her body heat, so she was sunk in to her ears, and as death had forfeited her natural heat, the warmed slush had iced up around her and now crusted in the fibers of her red sweater.

"Female, mid-to late-twenties. Time of death could be last evening," Elaine reported in her usual detached manner. She held a camera and had likely already snapped a few shots. "Didn't want to move the body for closer inspection until you arrived, Cash. You call in the BCA?"

"On their way. We can continue processing the crime scene. The BCA will help, if necessary. Last night, eh?"

"I suspect she was dumped here around midnightish."

Jason met Alex's gaze, above which the officer's brow quirked. They both tended to share a silent snicker at Elaine's frequent use of *ish* tacked to the end of words when she couldn't be exact.

"How do you know she was—" Jason drew his gaze from the body and up the slight ditch incline to the gravel road. The marks from a body sliding over the snow were obvious. "Right. Dumped."

Jason studied the ground, noting the footprints, which were obviously from Elaine's and Alex's boots, as they'd remained only on this side of the body. They hadn't contaminated the crime scene. That was Elaine's forte: meticulous forensics.

Jason walked a wide circle around the victim's head and up the ditch to the road. As he did so, Elaine snapped away, documenting every detail of the scene with photographs. Though they were still within city limits, this was not a main road. Rather, it was one of four that left the town and either dead-ended or led deeper north into the Boundary Waters Canoe Area Wilderness, a million-plus-acre natural reserve within the Superior National Forest that hugged the Canadian border. The only people who used this road were two families who both lived about ten miles out of Frost Falls. The gravel road showed no deep tracks in the mix of snow, ice and pebble, like if a vehicle were to take off quickly after disposing of evidence. But there were boot prints where the gravel segued into dead grass long packed down by snow.

Jason bent and decided they were a woman's boot prints for the narrowness.

"Marjorie said a woman called in the sighting?" Jason asked Alex.

"Yes, sir," Alex offered. "Call came from Susan Olson, who works at The Moose in the, er—ahem—back." If Alex hadn't been wearing a face mask, Jason felt sure he'd see him blush. The back of The Moose offered a low-class strip show on Saturday nights—basically, Susan and a few corny Halloween costumes that had fit her better back in high school. "Miss Olson was driving out to her aunt's place to check in on her when she saw something glint in the ditch."

Jason shuffled down into the ditch, avoiding Elaine as she stepped around the woman's head. "Evidence?" he asked Alex.

"Just the body and the clothing on it. No phone

or glasses or personal items that may have fallen out from a pocket. I'll bag the hands and head soon as Elaine gives me the go-ahead. Any tracks up there?"

"They're from the caller, I'm sure. But take pictures of the tracks, will you, Elaine? We'll have to see if Susan's fashion lends to size-eight Sorels, if my guess is correct."

"Of course. Nice thing about snow—it holds a good impression of boot tracks. I hope it's Ryan Bay with the BCA."

Jason cast her a look that didn't disguise his dislike for the guy for reasons he couldn't quite place. He'd only met him twice, but there was something about him.

Elaine noticed his crimped smirk and shrugged. "Guy's a looker. And he's easygoing. I can do what I need to do without him wanting to take charge."

"A looker, eh?"

There it was. She'd nailed his dislike in a word. A looker. What the hell did that mean? Wasn't as if handsome held any weight in this small town. Least not when a man was in the market to hook up. Again, no eligible women as far as a man's eye could see.

"You're still the sexiest police chief in St. Louis County, Cash." Elaine adjusted the lens on her camera. "But if you won't let me fix you up with my niece…"

The niece. She mentioned her every time they had occasion to work together. Blind dates gave Jason the creeps. His brother Joe had once gone on one. That woman had literally stalked him for weeks following. Yikes.

"Didn't you mention she was shortish?" Jason asked with a wink to Alex.

"Short girls need love, too, Jason." The five-foot-two-inch woman laughed. "Don't worry. I know she's not your type."

Jason squatted before the body, thinking that if Elaine actually did know his type— What was he thinking? Of course, she did. Along with everyone else in the county. The gossip in these parts spread as if it had its own high-speed internet service.

Focusing on the body, with a gloved hand he lifted the long black hair that had been covering the woman's face. Her skin was pale and blue. Her lips purple. Closed eyelids harbored frost on the lashes. No visible signs of struggle or blood. She was young. Pretty. He'd not seen her in Frost Falls before. And he had a good mental collection of all the faces in town. A visitor? She could have been murdered anywhere. The assailant may have driven from another town to place her here.

In the distance, the flash of headlights alerted all three at the same time.

"BCA," Elaine said. "We'll review the evidence with them and then bag the body."

"You'll transport the body to Duluth?" Jason asked.

"Yes," she said. "You going to follow me in for the autopsy?"

"You going to process it this morning?" Duluth was about an hour's drive to the east.

Elaine shook her head. "Probably not. But I will get to it after lunch. If you can meet me around oneish, that would work."

"Will do."

The white SUV bearing the BCA logo on the side door pulled up twenty feet from Alex's patrol car and idled. Looked like the driver was talking on the phone. Jason squinted. Couldn't make out who the driver was. A looker, eh? Why did that weird comment bother him?

It didn't. Really. He had a lot on his plate now. And he wasn't the type for jealously or even envy.

He glanced over the body of the unfamiliar woman. Pretty. And so young. It was a shame. "Any ID on her?"

"No, but she's probably Canadian," Elaine said.

Jason raised a brow at that surprising assessment.

Elaine bent and pushed aside the woman's hair with the tip of her penlight to reveal a tiny red tattoo of a maple leaf at the base of the victim's ear.

"Right." Jason frowned. "Are those ligature marks on her neck?"

"Yes." Elaine snapped a few close-up shots of the bruising now revealed on the woman's neck. "There's your signs of struggle right there. Poor thing." She replaced the victim's hair in the exact manner it had been lying and stood. "Looks like you just might have a murder case on your hands."

He'd suspected as much. Even though the weather could be treacherous and oftentimes deadly in the winter, the evidence screamed foul play.

"We'll get the BCA up to speed here, then I'm heading in to talk to Susan Olson," Jason said.

Jason had seen a lot, and he wasn't going to allow some psychopath to think he could get away with murder. As well, this was his first big case since his humiliating demotion from the CIA. The timing was either laughable or fortuitous, depending on how he looked at it. Because he'd just received notice that the police station had been marked for budget cuts. In all likelihood, it would close in March and Frost Falls would send all their dispatch calls through the county. The tiny town couldn't afford to pay Jason's meager salary anymore. But the notice had also mentioned it wasn't necessary to employ someone who was merely a town babysitter and not involved in real criminal procedures.

That one had cut deep. He was not a babysitter. Sure, he'd taken this job out of desperation. Getting ousted from the CIA was not a man's finest moment. Yet he had made this job his own. And he did have a lot on his plate, what with the domestic abuse calls, the poaching and— the public nudity.

Time to prove he wasn't incompetent to all those who were watching and taking notes. And with any luck? He might earn back his pride and a second chance.

Chapter Two

Nine a.m. on a lazy Sunday. Most of the Frost Falls inhabitants were at church in the neighboring town or sat at The Moose noshing on waffles and bacon. Most, but not all.

Susan Olson yawned and scrubbed a hand over her long, tangled red hair. Her eyes were smeared with dark eye makeup, toward her temple. She wore a Black T-shirt and bright pink sweatpants. They might have graduated the same year, but Jason had been born and raised in Crooked Creek, a town sixty miles west from here. Susan had lived in Frost Falls all her life.

Another yawn preceded "Really? Do you know what time it is, Chief Cash?"

"I do," Jason reported. He turned his head to block the wind that whipped at the front of the house. "Heard you found something interesting this morning."

"I knew you'd be stopping by. Just thought it would be at a decent hour. Come in."

Jason stepped inside the tiny rambler that might have been built in the '40s. It boasted green shag carpeting in the front living area; the walls were painted pink and—did they have glitter on them? He stayed on the rug before the door. His boot soles were packed with snow.

"Just have a few questions, then you can head back to bed," he said. "I know Saturdays are your busy night. Hate to bother you, but a woman has been murdered."

"She was murdered?" Susan's eyes opened wider. She clutched her gut and searched the floor. "I thought maybe she just died from, like, frostbite or something. Oh my God. I remember her. I mean, I didn't touch the body, but I did see her face this morning. I always run to check on my aunt Sunday mornings, even though I'm so raging tired after my shift."

"You..." Jason leaned forward, making sure he'd heard correctly. He tugged out the little notebook he always carried from inside his coat. Pen at the ready, he asked, "Remember her? The woman in the ditch?"

"Her and three others. It was Lisa Powell's clique. Must have been someone's birthday. They were loaded and loose last night. But the woman in the ditch didn't look familiar to me. I mean, I don't think she was from around here. It's not difficult to know all the locals."

Jason nodded and wrote down the information.

"She tipped me a ten," Susan said with a curl of a smile. "Doesn't happen often, let me tell you. The people in this town are so stingy."

"She was with Lisa Powell, and—do you know the names of the other two?"

"Hannah Lindsey and, oh, some older woman. Might have been one of their mothers. They are all older than me, don't ya know." She tilted out a hip and fluffed back her hair with a sweep of hand. "Must be in their late thirties, for heaven's sake."

Jason placed Susan at around thirty, same as him.

"Not an issue right now," Jason said. "How long were the women in The Moose? Did they all leave together? Who else was watching your performance?"

Susan yawned. "That's a lot of questions, Cash."

"I know. You got coffee?"

"I do, but I really don't want to wake up that much. I usually sleep until four on Sundays. Do we have to do this now?"

"We do. You'll remember much more detail now as opposed to later. And I have an appointment in Duluth in a few hours I can't miss."

Susan sighed and dropped her shoulders. "Fine. I got one of those fancy coffee machines for Christmas from my boyfriend. I'll make you a cup. Kick off your wet boots before you walk on my carpet, will you, Cash?"

"Will do."

Jason toed off his boots, then followed Susan into the kitchen, where a strange menagerie of pigs wearing sunglasses decorated every surface—all the dishware and even the light fixtures.

YVETTE LASALLE WANDERED down the tight aisles in the small grocery store set smack-dab in the center of Main Street in Frost Falls. The ice on her black hair that had sneaked out from under her knit cap melted and trickled down her neck. If she didn't zip up and wrap her scarf tight when she went outside, that trickle would freeze and— *Dieu.*

Why Minnesota? Of all the places in the world. And to make life less pleasant, it was January. The temperature had not been out of the teens since she had arrived. Sure, they got snow and cold in France. But not so utterly brutal. This place was not meant for human survival. Seriously.

But survive she would. If this was a test, she intended to ace it, as she did with any challenge.

This little store, called Olson's Oasis, sold basic food items, some toiletries, fishing bait and tackle (because crazy people drilled holes on the lake ice and actually fished in this weather), and plenty of cheap beer. A Laundromat was set off behind the freezer section. It boasted two washers and one semiworking dryer. The store was also the hub for deliveries, since the UPS service apparently didn't venture beyond Main Street.

Frost Falls was a virtual no-man's land. The last vestige of civilization before the massive Superior National Forest that capped the state and embraced the land with flora, fauna and so many lakes. This tiny town reminded Yvette of the village where her grandparents had lived in the South of France. Except Frost Falls had more snow. So. Much. Snow.

"Survival," she muttered with determination, but then rolled her eyes. She never would have dreamed a vacation from her job in gorgeous Lyon would require more stamina than that actual job. Mental stamina, that was.

But this wasn't a vacation.

Something called lutefisk sat wrapped in plastic behind the freezer-case glass. Vacillating on whether to try the curious fish, she shook her head. The curing process had something to do with soaking the fish in lye, if she recalled correctly from a conversation with the store's proprietor last week. It was a traditional Nordic dish that the locals apparently devoured slathered in melted butter.

Not for her.

Fresh veggies and fruits were not to be had this time of year, so Yvette subsisted on frozen dinners and prepackaged salads from the refrigerator case.

Her boss at Interpol, Jacques Patron, would call any day now. *Time to come home, Amelie. The coast is clear.* Every day she hoped for that call.

Unless he'd already tried her. She had gotten a strange hang-up call right before entering the store. The number had been blocked, but when she'd answered, the male voice had asked, "Yvette?" She'd automatically answered, "Yes," and then the connection had clicked off.

Wrong numbers generally didn't know the names of those they were misdialing. And an assumed name, at that. Had it been Jacques? Hadn't sounded like him. But he'd only said her name. Hard to determine identity from one word. Impossible to call back with the unknown number. And would her boss have used her cover name or her real name?

The call was not something to take lightly. But she couldn't simply call up Interpol and ask them for a trace. She was supposed to be dark. She and her boss were the only people aware of her location right now. She'd try her boss's number when she returned to the cabin.

Tossing a bag of frozen peas into her plastic basket, she turned down the aisle and inspected the bread selections. Not a crispy, crusty baguette to be found. But something called Tasty White seemed to be the bestseller. She dropped a limp loaf in her basket. She might be able to disguise the processed taste with the rhubarb jam that she'd found in a welcome gift basket when she'd arrived at the rental cabin.

When the bell above the store's entrance clanged,

she peered over the low shelves. A couple of teenage boys dressed in outdoor gear and helmets joked about the rabbit they'd chased with their snowmobiles on the ride into town.

Town? More like a destitute village with a grocery/post office/fish and tackle shop/Laundromat, and a bar/diner/strip joint—yes, The Moose diner offered "pleasure chats" and "sensual dancing" in the far back corner after 10:00 p.m. on Saturday nights. The diner did dish up a hearty meal, though, and Yvette's stomach was growling.

Her gaze averted from the boys and focused beyond the front door and out the frost-glazed window. Had that black SUV been parked before The Moose when she'd arrived? It looked too clean. Not a beat-up rust bucket like most of the locals drove. And it wasn't dusted with a grayish coating of deicing salt that they seemed to sprinkle on their roads more than their meals around here. She couldn't see the license plates to determine if it was a rental.

Yvette was alert for something she felt was imminent but was unable to say exactly what that could be. It reminded her of when she'd worked in the field. A field operative had to stay on her toes and be constantly aware of her surroundings, both physical and auditory. A wise state to embrace, especially in a town not her own.

She'd take a closer look at the SUV after she'd purchased her groceries.

The teenagers paid for energy drinks and left the store in a spill of laughter. Making her way to the checkout, Yvette set her basket on the counter.

"Bonjour, Yvette." Colette, the shop owner, a Canadian expatriate Yvette had bonded with because she spoke fluent French, fussed with the frilled pink polka-dot apron she wore over a slim-fitting black turtleneck and slacks. "Twenty dollars will do it."

Surely the bill was thirty or more.

Yvette nodded, unaccustomed to kindnesses, yet receiving such generosity felt like a warm summer breeze brushing her icy neck. Very much needed lately.

She handed over the money. Colette packed up her provisions and helped Yvette fit it all into the backpack she brought along for such trips. She looked forward to riding the snowmobile into town for twice-weekly grocery trips. And today, despite the single-digit temperature, boasted bright white sunshine. A girl could not ignore fresh air and the beautiful landscape. She always brought along her camera and stopped often to snapshots. It was a good cover for an agent, but photography had also always been a hobby she'd wanted to take to the next level.

"Those wool leggings look *très chic* on you," Colette commented, with a slide of her gaze down Yvette's legs. "But you really do need to wear snow pants if you're snowmobiling in this weather."

"I've got on layers." Yvette waggled a leg. The heavy boots she wore were edged with fake fur, and the leggings were spotted with white snowflakes on a blue background. Beneath, she wore thermal long johns, an item of clothing she hadn't been aware existed until she'd arrived here in the tundra. A quilted down coat topped it all.

Fitting the backpack over her shoulders, she paused at the door while Colette walked around the counter and met her with a zip up of her waterproof coat and a tug at her scarf (which happened to match her leggings—score one for fashion).

"You don't have a helmet to keep your ears warm?" Colette asked. She eyed Yvette's knit cap with the bobble of red pom-pom on the top. "You foreigners. I'm surprised your ears don't drop off with frostbite. It's colder than a polar bear's toenails out there. And with the wind chill? *Uff da*." The woman shuddered.

"Don't you mean *mon Dieu*?" Yvette countered.

Colette laughed. "Minnesota has gotten into my blood, *chère*. It's *uff da* here. Want me to order a helmet for you?" She tapped the pom-pom. "We order directly from the Arctic Cat supplier in Duluth. Takes only a day or two. And some are even electronic so you can turn on the heat and listen to music."

"Sounds perfect. The helmet provided by the cabin is too big for me and tends to twist and block my vision. Thanks, Colette."

"You heading across the street for a bite to eat? I see the chief's snowmobile just pulled up. That is one fancy machine. And I'm not talking about the snowmobile."

"The chief?" Yvette glanced across the way. "You mean a police chief? What's up?"

"Nothing of concern, I'm sure. It's just, have you met Chief Jason Cash?"

"Should I?"

Colette winked. "*Uff da*, girl, he's the hottest catch this side of the Canadian border. Young, handsome and cocky as hell. But none of the local girls can seem to turn his eye."

"I am hungry," Yvette said with a wistful glance across the street. For so many things she'd not had in almost two months. Sunshine. A buttery croissant. Conversation. Sex.

"Good girl. Tell the chief I said hello." Colette pushed the shop door open and virtually shoved Yvette out.

Bracing for the blast of cold, Yvette cursed how easily she had succumbed to the suggestion she hide out overseas until the heat on her blew over. Her boss had chosen this location and given her a cover identity. He hadn't told her exactly what it was that could implicate her, but she knew it had to do with her photographic memory. Thing was, she never really knew what some of the stuff that she worked on meant, as it was generally out of context and merely a list or scramble of information to her brain.

Boots crunching on the packed snow, she crossed the wide double-lane Main Street. A couple of pickup trucks with snow chains hugging the tires were parked before The Moose, as was one of the fanciest, most powerful snowmobiles she had seen. Walking by it, she forgot about the mysterious SUV she'd noticed earlier and instead took in the sleek black snowmobile dashed with neon-green embellishments. The body was like a blade, streamlined for speed.

The owner was handsome, eh? And single?

She wasn't looking for romance, that was for sure. But a woman could not survive on staticky rerun episodes of *Sex and the City* and her vibrator alone. Might as well *give the man a gander*, as she'd heard people say in these parts.

But for the official record, she was just here for the food.

Chapter Three

Jason took in the woman who sat before the diner counter. Two stools separated them. After setting a backpack on the floor, she'd pulled off a knit cap to let loose a spill of long black hair. Unzipping her coat halfway revealed a blue-and-white wool sweater that featured snowflakes and reindeer. Looked like one of Marjorie's knitted projects. Jason had one of those ugly sweaters—it featured a moose and possibly moose tracks (because he could never be sure it wasn't moose scat)—but he wore it proudly because someone had made it especially for him.

The woman at the counter was not a resident of Frost Falls. And today, of all days, he was particularly alert to strangers. This morning had brought a dead stranger onto his radar. Lunch had found him standing over an autopsy of the same woman. When driving back to Main Street, he'd sighted a shiny SUV that did not belong to a local. He'd run a plate check. Belonged to a Duluth resident. No police record or accidents reported. Worked for Perkins. Probably in town visiting friends.

And now Miss America was sitting ever so close.

She ordered mint tea and the club sandwich with extra bacon. The waitress winked and commented that she was glad to finally use up the tea she'd had stashed under the counter for years.

Jason noted the woman's cringe when she heard the date of the tea, and he chuckled.

"Not many tea drinkers in these parts," he said. "I haven't seen you in The Moose. You passing through Frost Falls?"

"In a means, yes," she said with an accent that sounded familiar to Jason.

She was an exotic beauty. Her skin tone was olive, and her features were narrow. Bright blue eyes twinkled beneath delicate curved black brows. She didn't fit the standard profile of the Scandinavians who populated a good portion of Minnesota's frozen tundra. Gorgeous, too, far prettier than most. And she didn't appear to be wearing a lick of makeup. Something about natural red lips...

Jason shook off a bittersweet memory of red lips and sly winks. Weird that he hadn't heard about this beautiful woman from the town's gossip mill. He turned on the stool to face her. "Name's Jason Cash," he offered. "I'm the town's chief of police."

For another few months, at least. If and when he lost this job, what would he have to show for his years of service to both his country and this small town?

Not a hell of a lot.

"Nice to meet you, Chief Cash. I'm Yvette La-Salle. I'm not exactly passing through this cozy town. I've been here a few weeks. For a, um, vacation. Decided to stop in the diner today because I was across the street making a grocery run."

"LaSalle." Must be French Canadian. Nix the Miss America idea, and replace it with…hmm… Her tone didn't seem to possess the rugged edge the Canadian accent offered. Interesting. And come to think of it, he had heard Marjorie mention something about a newcomer sitting in The Moose last week. Why had Marjorie failed to point out how drop-dead beautiful the woman was? Her gossip was usually much more on point. "I'm glad our paths crossed today."

The waitress set Yvette's plate and tea before her.

"Mind if I slide over?" Jason asked. "Then we don't have to yell across the room at one another."

"Go ahead." She pulled a strip of bacon out of the sandwich and munched the crispy slice. "Mmm, meat, how I have missed you."

"You go off meat for some crazy reason?"

"I am a vegetarian," she said, prodding another bacon strip, then eyeing it disdainfully. "Or rather, was." She took a big bite of the sandwich. "*Mon Dieu*, that is so good!"

Miss France, he decided. He'd only been assigned a single two-day Parisian job while serving in the CIA. He knew a handful of French words, but beyond that, his capacity for learning foreign languages was nil.

"You must not order the tea very often, eh?"

She rolled her eyes. "I had a misguided craving. I think this'll be the last time I get tea here."

"Stick with the root beer," Jason said. "Root beer never lets a man down."

"Sounds like a personal issue to me, but to each his own. I like your snowmobile," she said. "The one parked out front, yes? It looks like a racing machine."

"Oh, it is." Jason's back straightened, and he hitched a proud smile in the direction of the powerful machine parked outside. "Could have been a professional racer. I love burning up the track. But I don't have the time. This job keeps me on call 24/7."

"I suppose there is a lot of crime in this sleepy little town." She tried to hide a smirk, but Jason caught it. A fall of dark hair hid half her eye. Oh, so sexy. And every part of him that should react warmed in appreciation.

The last time he'd felt all the right things about a woman had been two years ago in Italy.

And that had ended disastrously.

"Somcone has to keep the Peanut Gang in line," he offered.

"The Peanut Gang?"

"Bunch of old farts who think poaching wolves isn't harming the ecosystem. Idiots."

"I'm not afraid of wolves. I think they are beautiful animals."

Jason nodded. "They are. But I'll leave it to my brother, the wolf whisperer, to kneel on the ground and pet them. It's always best to be cautious around wild animals."

Yvette nodded, but then said, "I got a great shot of a moose last week. On film, that is."

"Is that so?"

"I've learned to snowshoe out in the forest behind the cabin. Always take my camera along."

"You should be careful. Those beasts look gawky, but a moose can run fast."

"Tell me about it. I was photographing the snow-laced birch trees and out of nowhere a moose charged through the deep snow. It was beautiful. But I'm cautious to check for big critters now when I venture out."

"You should stick to the trails. Safer."

"Safe is good, hmm?"

Jason almost responded with an immediate *yes*, but he sensed by her tone that she was angling for bigger fish. Were those thick lashes as soft as they looked? And did she prefer not so safe? Now that was his kind of woman.

"Depends," he said. "There's safe and then there's, hmm...wild?"

"*Wild* is not a word I'd ever place to anything in this town."

If that wasn't some wanting, repressed sexual desire in her sigh, Jason couldn't guess otherwise. She had been in Frost Falls a few weeks. Why had he never noticed her before? And could he hope Alex hadn't already hooked up with her?

"You, uh, like wild?" he asked.

"I do." She finished off one triangle of the sandwich, but from his side view Jason noticed her smile did not fade.

Oh, he liked the wild, too. In so many ways.

The waitress set his bill down before him. He did not put it on the station's expense account. He couldn't see asking the town to pay for his meals. And now with the closure notice hanging over his head, he wanted to be as frugal as possible with the city budget. Much as he didn't like sharing the investigation with the BCA—yes, Ryan Bay, the looker, had arrived in town—it was a good thing, considering they had the resources and the finances to serve the investigation properly. As soon as the final autopsy report arrived, Jason intended to meet with Bay at the station house and go over the evidence.

Reaching for her backpack, Yvette shuffled it on over her arms. Ready to head out so quickly? She still had half a sandwich on the plate. He couldn't let her leave. Not until he'd learned more, like where she was staying, and did she have a significant other? And did her hair actually gleam when it spilled across her shoulders?

Briefly, Jason frowned as memories of his early morning stop resurfaced. The deceased had long black hair and a beautiful face.

At that moment, his cell phone buzzed with a text. Elaine had ID'd the victim as Yvette Pearson.

"Yvette," he muttered and wrinkled a brow. That was a weird coincidence.

"Yes?"

He looked up and was met with a wondering blue gaze. He'd once fallen for a pair of blue eyes and a foreign accent—and life had changed drastically for him because of that distraction.

"You said my name?" she prompted.

"Huh? Oh. No. I mean, yes. Not you. It's a text." He quickly typed, Thanks for the info. Forward the final report to me and Ryan Bay. He tucked away the phone and said to the very much alive Yvette, "It's a case. Not you. Sorry. Police business."

She nodded. "Yvette is a common French name."

"You betcha. Lot of French Canadians living up in these parts."

"These parts." With a sigh, she glanced out the front window.

Jason noticed she eyed the black SUV parked across the street. The one that hailed from Duluth.

"Friend of yours?" he asked, with a nod out the window.

"You mean the owner of that SUV?" She shook her head. "Despite my sparkling personality, and a desperate desire for good conversation, I don't have any friends in this town. Other than Colette at the market. She's the only French-speaking person I've run into."

"You speak French? I was wondering about your accent."

"I'm from Lyon."

Lyon, eh? That was a major city in France.

"So, what is there to do in this town that is more interesting than Friday night at the Laundromat slash grocery store?" Yvette asked.

"Let's see…" Jason rubbed his jaw. "A guy could nosh on some of the amazing desserts they have here at The Moose. I have to admit, I'm a big fan of their pie. You want a slice before you rush off?"

"Much as I would love to, I'll have to pass. Wasn't as hungry as I thought I was." She pushed the plate forward to indicate she was finished. "But I won't rule out pie in my future," she said with a teasing tone. "What else you got?"

"Well, there is Netflix and chill," Jason suggested slyly.

"I don't understand."

"It means…uh…" A blush heated Jason's cheeks. Since when had his flirtation skills become so damned rusty? And awkward. Mercy, he was out of practice.

"More coffee, Jason?" the waitress asked.

Saved by the steamy brew. "No, thanks, I should get going. Marjorie is waiting for me back at the office to sign off on some...paperwork."

The last thing he wanted to do was let the cat out of the bag that a body had been found so close to town. On the other hand, he expected when Susan Olson next went on shift at the back of the diner, it wouldn't take long for word to spread.

He pulled out a twenty and laid it on the counter. "That should cover both our bills."

Yvette zipped up her jacket. "Thank you, Chief Cash. I'm going to look up Netflix and chill when I get home."

"You do that," he said. And when she learned it meant watching Netflix together, then making out? "I'm down the street at the redbrick building if you ever need me. Used to be a bustling station house, but now it's just me and dispatch."

"Keeping an eye on the Peanut Gang."

"You betcha."

He walked her to the restaurant door, and she pointed across the street where a snowmobile was parked before Olson's Oasis. It was an older model, similar to the one he'd once torn through ditches on when he was a teenager.

"That's me," she said.

"How far out do you live?" he asked.

"I'm renting. Here for a short stay. It's a cabin about five miles east. Lots of birch trees. Very secluded."

"Everything around here is secluded. You step out of town, you're in no-man's land. That's what I love about this place. And lots of powder."

"Powder?"

"Snow. When I'm not working, I spend my time on the cat, zooming through the powder. Er, *cat* is what some locals call the snowmobile. At least, those of us with an inclination to Arctic Cat sleds and racing."

"Ah, a thrill seeker?"

"You nailed it. You must be staying at the Birch Bower cabin?"

"Yes, that's the one."

Jason nodded. The owners rented the place out in the winter months while they vacationed in their Athens home. Nice place, Greece. Beautiful blue waters. Fascinating local culture. Ouzo in abundance. He'd nearly taken a bullet to the stomach there a few years ago. Good times.

"Thanks again," Yvette called as she walked away.

Feeling as though he wanted to give Yvette his phone number, Jason also suspected that would not be cool. Not yet. They'd only chatted ten minutes. So instead he watched her turn on her snowmobile and head off with a smile and a wave.

Besides, he knew where to find her now if he wanted to.

A glance to the SUV found it was still parked. Exhaust fumes indicated the engine was running. Hmm...

Jason strode across Main Street toward the SUV, boots crunching the snowpack. The vehicle shifted into gear and drove past him. It slowed at the stop sign at the east edge of town. And sat there. Yvette had crossed to the town's edge and taken a packed trail hugged by tall birch trees.

The thunder of Jason's heartbeats would not allow him to dismiss the SUV. It was almost as if the driver had been parked there, watching... Yvette?

He looked at his cell phone. Elaine's message read, Yvette Pearson.

As the very much alive Yvette LaSalle had said, it was a common French name. But two Yvettes in one small town? Both, apparently, visiting. And one of them dead?

Unable to shake the itchy feeling riding his spine, Jason returned to his snowmobile and pulled on his helmet. By the time he'd fired up the engine and headed down Main Street, the SUV had slowly moved toward the birch-lined road heading east. Yvette's direction.

Jason pulled up alongside the SUV, switched on the police flasher lights and signaled the driver to pull over. He did so and rolled down his window. The thirtysomething male wearing a tight gray skullcap and sunglasses tugged up a black turtleneck as the brisk air swept into the truck cab.

"Chief Jason Cash," Jason said as he approached the vehicle. A nine-millimeter Glock hugged his hip, but he didn't sense a need for it. Nor did he ever draw for a routine traffic stop. Not that this was a traffic stop.

"Hello, Officer," the man said with an obvious accent. Texan? A Southern drawl twanged his voice. "Is there a problem?"

"No problem. I've not seen you in Frost Falls before, and it is a small town. Like to introduce myself." He tugged off a glove and offered his hand to the man. The driver twisted and leaned out the window to shake his hand. A calm movement. Warm hand. But Jason couldn't see his eyes behind the mirrored lenses. "Your name?"

"Smith," he said easily. Which was the name Jason had gotten from the plate check. "I'm visiting the Boundary Waters tourist area. Just out for a drive. Beautiful day with the sunshine, yes?"

"You betcha."

Definitely a Texan accent. Fresh out of high school, Jason had served three years in the marines alongside a trio of Texans who had extolled their love for hot sauce whenever they were bored.

"You got some ID and vehicle registration, Smith?"

The man reached down beside him. Jason's

hackles tightened. He placed a hand over his gun handle. Smith produced a driver's license and, opening the glove compartment, shuffled around for a paper. He handed both over.

Hiding his relief that he hadn't had to draw against a dangerous suspect, Jason took the items and looked them over. It was a Minnesota license, not Texas, but people moved all the time. The name and address matched the vehicle registration. It also matched the info he'd gotten earlier. Thirty-seven years old. Brown hair. Brown eyes. Donor. A Duluth address. Hair was longer in the photo, but the man looked like he'd recently had a clipper cut.

"You a recent move to Minnesota?"

"Why do you ask?"

"There's not a lot of *uff da* in your accent."

The man chuckled. "Born and raised in Dallas. But I do enjoy the winters here."

"I gotta agree with you there. You must enjoy outdoor sports."

"Mostly taking in the sights."

"Uh-huh. You got the day off from work?" Jason asked.

"You bet."

"Duluth, eh?" Jason handed back the license. "Where do you work?"

"Perkins. Just off Highway 35 west."

Jason had eaten at that location before. So that checked out, too. In town to take in the scenery?

"Thank you, Mr. Smith. You should turn around here before the road gets too narrow," he said. "It's not for tourism. And it's also not a through road."

"I had no idea, Officer."

"That's part of my job. Making sure everyone stays on the straight and narrow."

The man furrowed his brows. And the fact he'd misnamed the Boundary Waters Canoe Area Wilderness gave Jason another prickle down his spine. A strange mistake for someone who should be familiar with the area.

"The Moose serves up some tasty meat loaf with buttered carrots," Jason offered. "Stop in before you head out of town."

"Thank you, Officer. I will. Is there anything else?"

"No. You can go ahead and turn around here. Road's still wide enough. But watch the ditch. The snowpack is loose. You'll catch a tire and have a hell of a time getting out. Tow service is kind of sketchy in these parts."

"Sure thing."

The window rolled up, and Jason walked back over to his snowmobile. The SUV sat for a bit, not making any motion to turn around. Clouds of exhaust formed at the muffler.

Jason sat on his cat and swung the driver a friendly wave. If he had been following Yvette, there was no way Jason was going to leave his post. And if the driver had known her, he would have mentioned he was following a friend. Maybe?

When the vehicle finally began to pull ahead, turn, back up, turn some more, then make the arc around to head back the way it had come, Jason again waved.

"Something up with Smith," he muttered.

He could generally spot a fake ID at a glance. The license had been legit. Everything checked out in the police database. But still, his Spidey senses tingled. Sure, Frost Falls got sightseers. The town's namesake, the falls, froze solid in the winter months. It attracted thrill seekers. And idiots.

But the man hadn't mentioned the falls specifically. And if that had been his destination, he should have headed out of town in the opposite direction.

Jason had met three strangers today. And one of them had been lying dead in a ditch. He wasn't going to let this one sit.

Firing up the cat, he headed back into town to keep an eye on Smith.

Chapter Four

Jason breezed into the station but didn't unzip his coat or stomp his boots. Marjorie had gotten used to his tromping in ice and snow and had laid down a rubber runner mat a year ago. She still complained about the mess, but when he'd given her a budget for a monthly rug cleaning, she'd settled.

That would all change soon enough. He wasn't sure how to tell her the station might be closed in March. He had to tell her. Maybe if he waited, it would never happen?

"There's a message," Marjorie started as he walked by.

"From the BCA?" Jason asked.

"No, Bay's in your office—"

He strode into his office and closed the door behind him. "Bay."

The agent was seated in the extra chair against the wall beneath a sixteen-point deer rack with a laptop open and his focus pinned to the screen. "Cash. Give me a minute."

"Minute's all you get. I'm investigating a murder. Have to get out there. Talk to people. Gather information."

Walking across the room, Jason pushed aside the shades to give him a view of Main Street. He'd seen Smith's SUV heading east toward Highway 35. The man had taken the hint.

On the other hand... He glanced down the street toward the gas station that sat at town's edge.

"They still renting snowcats from the gas station?" Jason called out to Marjorie.

"You betcha. Jason, do you want some krumkake?"

That invite turned his head. He strode back into the next room and eyed the plate of sweet treats Marjorie pointed to on the corner of her desk. Half a dozen delicate rolled sweets sat on a Corelle plate decorated around the circumference with green leaves (just like his mother's set). Krumkake were like crunchy crepes, but so light and delicious.

"You make those?" he asked.

"Of course. I use my grandmother's krumkake iron. They don't make those things anymore, don't ya know."

He grabbed one of the treats and bit into it, catching the inevitable crumbs with his other hand. Two more bites and it was gone. He grabbed another, then tugged out his notebook and tore out a few pages to hand to Marjorie. "Can you type up these notes I took while talking to Susan Olson?"

"Of course. I've already got a case file started. Elaine Hester forwarded the autopsy report for the woman in the ditch. I left a copy on your desk, and Bay's got a copy as well."

"Yeah, she texted me the name Yvette Pearson." Jason wandered back into his office and closed the door behind him.

Ryan Bay stood and set the laptop on Jason's desk. "I've got family info on the victim."

"Lives in a Minneapolis suburb," Jason said. Susan had been sure the women at the club the other night were from the Twin Cities, because one had worn a jacket with a high school logo embroidered on the sleeve. "Blaine?"

"Yes, Blaine. I've already contacted their police department so they can get in touch with the family."

"I've got a list of the deceased's friends I intend to question as soon as I step out of the station. But first, I'm going to head east and check on—"

"That pretty young woman you talked to in The Moose?" Marjorie asked as she entered with the plate of treats in hand.

Marjorie took his silence as the hint she needed it to be and, after handing him the plate, she left the office with a promise to get right to his notes.

Jason closed the office door again and nodded to Bay, who turned his laptop toward him. "Classic homicide. Ligature marks. Struggle bruises on forearms and DNA under fingernails."

"Yep, I was there for the autopsy. It was all very clean. Generally there's much more bruising on the body as the killer struggles to complete the unfamiliar—or unintended—task. Anger and aggression."

Bay shook his head and exhaled heavily. "You said you talked to the woman who found the body?"

"Yes, she gave me the names of the women the victim was last seen with. That's where I'm going next—"

"I thought there was a pretty young woman?" Bay said with a smirk.

"A..." Jason closed his eyes and shook his head. Marjorie really needed to stay out of his personal life. But the worst part of it was that she knew about his personal life before it tended to get personal. "Never mind," he said. "You don't want to question the victim's friends, do you?"

Bay tilted his head, a casual thought process taking place inside his perfectly coiffed head. He wore a suit, for some damn reason, and it looked like his fingernails had been manicured for the glossy shine. Was that what women found attractive? Yikes.

"Go for it," Bay said. "The locals are more likely to be comfortable talking to someone they know. When I consult on a case, I like to guide and keep track, but ultimately, this is your case,

Cash. I'm not going to trample on your turf. And I'm starving. I haven't eaten yet today."

"Then The Moose is your next stop." Jason picked up the documents Marjorie had left for him on his desk. "You staying in town?"

"There's no motel. Snow Lake has a halfway decent Best Western and free coffee."

"Not a problem. My office is yours. I'll let you know what I learn." Jason strode out and through the reception area, pleased that Bay was easygoing. Which would give him all the rope he required to control this investigation. He really needed this one. It was an opportunity to show the powers that be that he had what it took to manage real police work, and that the Frost Falls police force, as small as it was, was a necessity.

Instead of the snowmobile, he'd drive the Ford. He could use some warmth. Turning up the car heater to blast, Jason rolled down Main Street, the car tires crunching as if across Styrofoam as they moved over the packed snow. He loved that sound. It was hard to describe to anyone who didn't live on snow six months out of the year. To him it meant home.

From here he could see the small parking lot in front of the gas station. No business name on the broken red-and-white sign above the station. It had been called just "gas station" forever, according to an elder member of the town.

And yet, when Jason cruised closer to the gas

station, he saw the black SUV parked around the back side of the white cinder-block building. It was the one licensed to James Smith.

"What the hell?"

He pulled into the station lot. Hopping out of the truck and blowing out a breath that condensed to a fog, Jason quickened his pace into the station.

"Afternoon, Cash," the owner said from his easy chair placed on a dais behind the cash register. Easier to see out the window and watch the town's goings-on from that height.

"You rent out any cats this afternoon, Rusty?"

"I just did, not ten minutes ago. Local fellow."

"Local?"

"Well, you know, he mentioned he was from Duluth. That's local."

It was. The port city that sat on Lake Superior was an hour's drive east and within the St. Louis County lines.

"Gave him directions to the falls and told him to stick to the trails," Rusty said, "but I think he went east. Idiot. Your brother still with the State Patrol?"

"Justin? Yep. He's stationed near the Canadian border right now. Big drug-surveillance op going on."

"Those marijuana farms." Rusty shook his head.

"You betcha. What was the name of the renter?"

Rusty tapped a crinkled piece of paper hanging from a clipboard to the right of the register. "Smith. Sounded foreign. And not Canadian foreign. He was a mite different. Like those duck hunters they got on that television show."

"Thanks, Rusty. Gotta go."

Jason made haste to the truck, and before the door was even closed he pulled out onto the main road and turned to hit the eastbound road that led to the Birch Bower cabin. It was only five miles out, but with each mile the forest thickened and hugged closer on both sides of the narrowing road. It was as desolate as a place could get so close to a small town.

As he drove down the gravel road that the plow only tackled every Monday morning, he noted the snowmobile tracks lain down on the road shoulder. A couple of them. Freshly impressed into the crusted snowpack. One set must belong to Yvette. The other?

"Smith."

In his next thought, Jason wondered if he were getting worked up over nothing. No. She'd said she didn't know anyone in town. And yet she had looked at the SUV for a while.

Didn't feel right to Jason. And if he'd learned anything over the years, it was to trust his intuition.

ONE OF THE reasons Yvette hadn't minded leaving home for a while was that she'd been questioning her job choice for some time now. She'd never been fooled that being a field operative for an international security agency was glamourous or even 24/7 action-adventure. The job could be tedious at times. Mildly adrenalizing, at best. Most people associated spies with glamour and blockbuster movies. In truth, the average agent spent more time doing boring surveillance than the few minutes of contact with a suspect that might provide that thrill of action.

Yet beyond the intrigue and danger, a surprising moral struggle had presented itself to her when she was faced with pulling the trigger on a human target. She was not a woman prone to crying fits. And yet, the tears had threatened when she'd been standing in the field, gun aimed at a person and—she'd been unable to pull the trigger. Human life meant something to her. Even if the human she had been charged to fire at was a criminal who had committed vile crimes. She'd not expected to only realize such moral leanings until the heat of the moment, but that pause had changed her life irreversibly.

She asked for a change of pace and had, thankfully, been allowed to continue her work in data tech. A job that didn't fulfill her in any tangible manner. It had become an endless stream of data on the computer screen.

Now seclusion in a snow-covered cabin offered an excellent time to consider her future. Did she really want to continue on this career path? Days ago, she'd started a list of pros and cons regarding her current employer.

Yvette tapped the pen beside her temple as she delved deep for another pro. She felt it necessary to write down the good as well as the bad reasons to stay or leave. Solid and tangible. Easy to review. Difficult to deny once inked on paper. Because she'd followed in her parents' footsteps, career-wise. Had thought she was cut out for the gritty hard-core work it required.

Yet to her surprise, the desk job had, strangely, become more dangerous than fieldwork. She had seen something on the computer screen that she was not supposed to see. She just didn't know what that something was, because it had been a list, and perhaps even coded.

Setting aside the pros and cons list and getting up to stretch, she exhaled. She'd been working on the list for an hour while listening to the wind whip against the exterior timber walls. A blizzard was forecast.

"Joy," she muttered mirthlessly and wandered into the kitchen.

No thought cells could operate without a healthy dose of chocolate. Plucking a mug out of the cupboard, she then filled the teapot with water and set that on the stove burner.

She shook the packet of hot chocolate mix into the mug. Right now, she needed a heat injection.

Her toes were freezing, even though she wore two layers of socks. And her fingers felt like ice. She'd turned up the heater upon returning from the grocery run, but it didn't want to go any higher than seventy-four degrees.

With the wind scraping across the windows, she felt as if she sat in a wooden icebox. A glance to the fireplace made her sigh. A woodpile sat neatly stacked outside and behind the house. The owners had suggested she carry some in before too much snow fell, but she'd not done that. After she'd fortified her chilled bones with hot chocolate, she'd have to bundle up and bring out the ax to chip the frozen logs apart. The night demanded a toasty fire in the hearth.

The teapot whistled, and she poured the steaming water into the mug. Oh, how she missed the thick, dark chocolate drink served exclusively by the French tea shop Angelina. Unfortunately, the shop hadn't come to Lyon, but she visited Paris often enough and stocked up when there.

Tilting back the oversweet chocolate drink, she sighed and took a moment to savor the heat filling her belly. Who would have thought she could enjoy a moment of warmth so thoroughly? It was a different kind of warmth from the one she'd felt sitting in the diner talking to the chief of police. Colette had been spot on regarding her assessment of the man. He was a handsome one. He'd seemed about her age, too.

A knock on the front door startled her. That was—not weird. The postman knocked every day with her mail in hand. Not that she got personal mail. It was always ads and flyers for retirement homes. But she did appreciate his smile and some chat. He often asked if she was comfy and did she like fruitcake? His wife had extra. Yvette always declined with the knowledge that fruitcake was not a culinary treat.

Yet something stopped her from approaching the door. She still couldn't erase the police chief's question about the mysterious SUV. It had seemed out of place in the small town. And she was no woman to ignore the suspicious.

Grasping a pen from the kitchen counter, Yvette fit the heavy steel object into her curled fingers, then walked cautiously over to the door. She stood there a moment, staring at the unfinished pine wood that formed the solid barrier. There was no peephole.

"Who is it?" she called.

"Delivery," answered back. "Is your name… Yvette?"

"Yes, but…" Yvette frowned. It was her cover name. She hadn't ordered anything. And she'd only this morning asked Colette to order the helmet.

"It's from The Moose," the man said. "You didn't order anything?"

"No," she called back. "It's food? Who sent it?"

A pause, and then, "Note says it's from a new friend."

A new friend? And The Moose? But she'd just—had the police chief sent her a gift? Of food? They had discussed pie. How nice of him. And if it was a flirtatious move, she was all in.

Yvette opened the door.

The man standing on the snow-dusted front stoop was tall and dressed all in black, including the black face mask he wore that concealed all but his eyes. He growled and lunged for her. He fit his bare hands about her throat, and Yvette stumbled backward.

Chapter Five

Jason ran in through the open doorway and encountered a struggle. In front of the floor-to-ceiling windows that overlooked a snow-frosted copse of maples, he witnessed a man shove a woman—Yvette LaSalle—against the wall. Her painful grunt fired anger in Jason's veins. He dashed over a fallen chair and toward the struggling duo.

Suddenly, Yvette swept her hand forcefully backward, her elbow colliding with the attacker's neck. She twisted and plunged a fist against his head. The man—Smith—yelped and gripped his bleeding scalp.

Jason charged across the room. With a swift right hook, he connected under Smith's jaw and knocked him out cold. The man dropped to his side, sprawling on the floor.

He spun around to find Yvette behind him, clutching a tactical pen in one hand. A fierce, huffing demeanor held her at the ready before him. Her stance declared she was prepared for more fight.

"It's okay," Jason reassured. "He's out."

She nodded, but her defensive pose remained. Impressive. She'd been terrorized. The adrenaline must be coursing through her like a snowmobile around a racetrack.

"That was— You were—incredible." Jason finally found the right words. "You are certainly no damsel."

"No, I'm not." She winced, but lifted her chin. "He was strong. Stronger than…"

Jason sensed the adrenaline was beginning to rapidly drop from the high that had served her the strength to defend herself. Yvette's body began to shake. He rushed over and took her in his arms.

"It's okay." He hugged her firmly, pressing his face against the crown of her head. She smelled like salt and summer. A sweep of soft hair tickled his nose. His thundering heartbeats thudded loudly. But was it from the moment of attack, or from the surprising feeling of holding a trembling woman in his arms? Mercy. She had reacted unexpectedly bravely. And her sudden surge of strength may have saved her life.

"You did good, Yvette. Guy's out like a light." For now. "I need to cuff him. Can I let you go?"

She nodded against his chest, though her fingers clung to his biceps, unwilling to relent. Jason stepped back but bowed to check her gaze. When she offered him a wincing smile, he slowly extracted himself from her grip. She wasn't going to faint. Not this brave woman.

Digging out the cuffs from his jacket, he bent to secure the suspect's hands behind his back.

"You know this guy?" he asked over his shoulder.

"No. Do you?"

"He's the guy from the black SUV."

"I told you I didn't know him when you asked in the diner."

"I know, but he put up my hackles. I pinned him for something more than a guy taking in the scenery. He was following you."

"He was? How did you— Why didn't you stop him before he got here?"

"I thought I had." Jason stood and grabbed the back of a fallen chair and righted it. He lifted a boot, realizing the papers scattered on the floor were wet and torn. No saving them. "I didn't expect him to rent a snowmobile and go after you. Why was he after you?"

"We've been over this, Chief Cash. I've never met him."

"How did he get inside the cabin?"

"I, uh…" She clutched her throat. Her fingers visibly shook. "Opened the door."

Jason stopped an admonishing retort and instead asked carefully, "You always let strangers inside?"

"He said he had a delivery from The Moose.

Why did you talk to him in town? What made you wonder about him?"

"He looked suspicious. We've got an active investigation going on and—"

"Investigation? Like what? A man attacking women?"

She was close. Jason never gave out details of an ongoing investigation. Was the man on the floor the one who had murdered the woman he'd found in the ditch this morning? He had been attempting to strangle Yvette. The one in the ditch had died by strangulation. And Jason never subscribed to coincidence.

Yet would a stalker, or even some sort of serial strangler, have allowed a woman to get the upper hand with a weapon so simple as a tactical pen?

As well, how many seemingly innocent women vacationing in a secluded cabin carried a tactical pen on them? It was a self-defense weapon that most did not know about or bother to keep close enough to use.

"That's a handy thing, isn't it?" He gestured to the rugged black steel pen she still held.

She clutched it against her chest and lifted her chin. "I never go anywhere without it. It's something I was trained—"

"You've taken self-defense training?"

When she looked up quickly, as if he'd discovered a secret, a moment of clarity softened her features, then she shrugged. "Like you said, I'm not a damsel."

"I guess not. But didn't the training class teach you never to open the door to a stranger?"

Another shrug. She avoided his gaze, as well. Hmm...

"Are you going to get him out of here?" she asked with a gesture to the fallen attacker.

"I'll give Officer Larson a call." Jason wasn't ready to leave without asking more questions. And he couldn't do that and watch the perp at the same time. "You sure you're okay?"

"Of course I am," she said a little too quickly. Then a sweep of her hand through her hair preceded a hefty sigh. "But if you'll excuse me, I'm going to step into the, uh...little girls' room for a bit."

"Go ahead. I won't leave until this guy is out of your hair." He tugged out his phone and dialed up dispatch. He and Alex alternated shifts, but both were on call 24/7. And he'd rather have him come and assist than the lackadaisical Ryan Bay.

YVETTE CLOSED THE bathroom door behind her and exhaled. Her shoulders hit the door. She caught her head in a palm. Her entire body shook, but she didn't cry. She sank, bending her knees, until she sat on the tiled floor.

That man could have killed her.

She was thankful that the police chief was here

and had rescued her in the nick of time. But a retreat to the bathroom had been necessary. She hadn't wanted him to see her break down. And what was this shaking about? She was better than this—trained for such encounters, and well able to defend herself against some of the strongest attackers.

Yet she hadn't panicked when he'd come at her. She had done her best to protect herself from what could have been a terrible outcome. Because the man had had his hands about her neck and his thumbs pressed against her larynx. She'd gasped and had felt her lungs tighten.

It had been over a year since she'd worked as a field agent and had exercised her defense skills. Had she gotten so out of shape and ineffective in such a short time?

"Get it together, Amelie," she whispered. "Why did this happen?"

Because Amelie Desauliniers had been sent out of the country to hide under an assumed identity. But hide from whom or what hadn't been made clear to her. Surely this hadn't been a random attack. And yet she was undercover. Dark. Who had found her?

A quiet knock on the door preceded "Yvette? You okay in there?"

She closed her eyes.

"Yvette?"

"Oh." Despite embracing the name, it just

didn't click sometimes. As well, she'd have to form words to reassure the police chief. Inhaling a quiet sniffle, she said, "Sorry. Yes, give me a few minutes. I'm a little shaken."

"Thought you might be. I'll be out in the living room. Another officer is on the way to pick up the perp."

She waited until his boots echoed away down the hall. Amelie stood and walked to the sink. Twisting on the water spigot, she splashed her face but let out a gasp. She would never get used to the fact the water took a good three or four minutes to reach room temperature. But the frigid water did work to shock away her tears.

Pressing a towel over her face to dry it, she then nodded at her reflection. The agent she had once been must be tugged out of retirement. For survival purposes. "I can do this."

But she couldn't ask the sexy police chief for help. Her stay here in Minnesota was classified. And not knowing what she knew had suddenly become a detriment. She had to speak with her boss. And soon.

Returning to the living room, she walked around the prone body on the floor. The attacker was coming to, groaning. Another knock on the door sounded. Amelie jumped. A pair of gentle, warm hands settled onto her shoulder.

"It's Alex, my assistant," Chief Cash reassured her in a deep voice that hinted at the strength she desperately required. "Why don't you sit on the couch." He touched her upper arm, and she winced. "Looks like you got hurt. Your sweater is torn. I'll take a look after I get the perp out of here."

He opened the door, and the waiting police officer nodded and introduced himself to her as Amelie settled onto the couch. He was tall and attractive. Not handsome sexy, more like boy-band cute. The thought summoned her out of the heavy tension that had made her clutch the tactical pen. She set the pen on the coffee table and inspected her sweater.

She'd been hurt? She hadn't noticed while shivering in the bathroom. Yet now that Jason had pointed it out, she felt the sting of pain in her biceps. Her sweater was torn and bloody. And...yes, the pointed tip of the pen was bloodied, so she'd caused her attacker some damage.

The two men picked up the suspect by his upper arms. He growled and struggled against the handcuffs. Both officers had to move him out of the cabin, kicking and gyrating across the threshold. As they exited, the attacker called, "I will be back for you!"

Amelie swore and turned to clasp her arms about her legs, pulling them tight against her chest. Her heart thudded up to her throat.

She knew something dangerous. It was locked away in her brain, and only she possessed the key to dredge out the information.

Chapter Six

Standing on the front stoop, Jason watched Alex back the patrol car out of the double-wide drive. Alex gave him a thumbs-up as he headed toward town. He'd secure the perp behind bars, and Ryan Bay could help book him and start an interrogation.

He leaned back inside the cabin and called, "I'm going to take a look around the cabin and surrounding area. Look for clues. You okay alone for a bit?"

"Of course."

The answer was the right one, but it sounded shaky. To be expected.

"Give me half an hour. I'll stay close. If you need me, just shout out the door."

Wind and snow crystals scoured Jason's face as he rounded the side of the cabin, following the faint traces of boot prints that were neither his nor did they belong to a female. Another hour of wind and the tracks would be gone.

An outjut of stacked pine logs formed a two-sided protection from the wind and elements for the generator. He lifted the blue tarp cover and looked over the machine. Some snow had drifted up about the base, but it all looked in working order. He might turn it on to check it out, but it was windy, and he wanted to beat the storm before it erased all evidence Smith had left behind.

Picking up his pace through a foot of fluffy, dry snow, Jason passed the detached double garage behind the cabin. He sighted sunken boot prints. They did not reveal sole design because the snow and wind had already filled them, but he could see they walked toward the cabin. Scanning ahead, he noticed the line of tracks and veered toward the line of white-paper birches that edged a forest fifty yards ahead. The footprints disappeared for ten feet, but then he could pick up the sunken smooth imprint when he flashed the flashlight beam over it. But he didn't need the tracks when he spied the snowmobile in the woods.

Hastening his steps, he entered the woods, which blocked the wind. Thankful for that reprieve, he huffed out a breath. The cold was something he was accustomed to, but when the wind beat directly at his face, it took a man's breath away.

Tromping over fallen branches and loose snow made footing difficult. The snowmobile still had the keys in the ignition. A rental sticker on the hood told him it had come from the gas station. Smith had likely intended to do the deed and head back to the snowmobile for a quick getaway.

Jason sat on the snow-dusted vinyl seat cushion and flashed the light beam about the sled. The gas station kept its rental machines in tip-top condition, even if they were decades old. This one was fully gassed up. The seat was comfy and not torn. The outer fiberglass hood was not scuffed, save for a small crack where the windshield connected.

The footprints, which now he could plainly see were from cowboy boots, took off from the sled and walked straight on toward the cabin—no pacing about the vehicle, deciding to get up his courage. The man had been focused, set on his task. He'd wanted to get at this second Yvette.

Had it been the same man coming after yet another Yvette? The implications pointed toward some type of serial stalker. A man obsessed with Yvettes?

He tipped open the cover of the small supply box on the back of the seat cushion. Nothing inside. If the man had intended to use a weapon against Yvette, he would have brought it along with him into the cabin. Jason hadn't removed any weapons from him when cuffing him and patting him down.

Jason flipped the box cover shut. He would check on Yvette, and—hell, she had been bleeding.

BACK INSIDE THE CABIN, Jason kicked off his boots. When he wandered into the living room and sat next to Yvette on the couch, he sensed her shivers before seeing them. She was still frightened. The tactical pen lay on the pine coffee table. He would secure that as evidence.

"You were very brave," he said in his reassuring officer's tone. Something a guy cultivated with experience. "Can I look at your arm?"

She nodded but didn't speak as he carefully pulled away the torn knitted threads from her arm. There was a good amount of blood, but it looked like it might be road rash. Nothing deep. She must have rubbed against something rough when struggling with the perp. All the furniture in this cabin was fashioned from heavy, bare pine logs, so it was feasible she could have fallen against a chair leg or arm.

"I found the snowcat the perp drove out here in the woods. I'll have a tow come get it after the storm threat passes. I think you should come to town with me and have Marjorie, my dispatcher, look at that. Just to be safe. And I do need you to give me an official statement."

"I'm okay."

"Marjorie used to be a nurse," he encouraged.

"It's just a bruise. And I know you have questions—standard police procedure, and all that—"

"I really do need to talk to you while the incident is fresh in your mind. It's just odd. The guy was following you. He sat outside on Main Street, watched you walk across from the grocery store, stayed there while you had a bite to eat and then..." He sighed heavily.

"I've never seen that man before, Chief Cash."

"Then why did you let him inside the cabin?"

"I called out and he said he had a delivery and asked if my name was Yvette."

"A delivery?"

"Said it was from a new friend. I assumed it was from you. We *had* talked about pie."

"You thought I sent you pie?"

"It sounded reasonable at the time. I opened the door, and then he lunged. You arrived a minute or two later. *Merci Dieu.*"

"So he called you by name?"

She nodded.

"Your full name?"

Yvette thought about it a moment. "No, just my first. I did have the clarity to grab the tactical pen before answering the door."

"So you were suspicious."

"I was until he said the—er, my name. Then I believed he was a deliveryman."

"Right. So, he started to choke you immediately? Or did you have a conversation first?"

"No, he immediately went at me. I was able to struggle and move the two of us across the room toward the table, where you see the mess."

"Those papers on the floor…" Jason looked over her shoulder. "Important?"

"Uh, no. Just some journaling stuff. Why? You think he was after something of mine?"

"I don't know. You have to tell me."

"He didn't speak after I'd let him inside. Didn't ask for anything, like where my valuables were. I don't believe he was here to rob me. He wanted to hurt me. Possibly even…"

Jason nodded and tugged out his notebook to make a few notations.

"How many people know you're staying here?" he asked.

"One," she said, then offered him a shrug as if to apologize for that low number.

"No friends? Family?"

She shook her head, keeping her lips tight.

"Sounds kind of odd," he remarked. "Single woman off alone in a country foreign to her, and only one person knows about it? Boyfriend?"

She shook her head again, choosing silence. A silence that niggled at Jason's trust. Why not provide the person's name without his prompting?

"Who knows you're here, Miss LaSalle?"

"Just my boss. This was a retreat," she added quickly. "A photography excursion. A last-minute decision sort of thing, so I didn't announce it to everyone I know. Just…got the time off I needed, and…here I am."

"Here you are. You work as a photographer?"

She nodded.

He wasn't buying it. Wouldn't a photographer have equipment? He hadn't noticed any cameras in the open-layout cabin. "Your boss is a photographer as well?"

She shrugged. "It's a hobby. I'm trying to expand my portfolio."

Jason closed his notebook and stuffed it inside his coat. "Anything else you want to tell me about what happened?"

"No."

"So he was only in the cabin a few minutes before I arrived?"

"Yes. Or it felt that long. I can't be sure, but I'd guess that's about as long as I'd last against someone so strong."

"Fine. I have to head in and help process the suspect." And he'd been on his way to talk with the victim's friends before the detour out here to the cabin.

"I'm going to call you in an hour," he said. "To check in with you. You should be safe now."

She nodded. "Thank you." She glanced to the papers strewn on the floor.

"Will you also promise not to open the door for anyone except the mailman?"

"That's a deal. Write down your number on one of those papers before you leave."

He stood and picked up a paper from the floor.

It was a lined notebook page. He read the header. "Pros and cons?"

"Just doing some journaling."

Wanting to read more, but respecting her privacy, he tugged the pen out of his coat and scribbled down his number on the back of the paper.

When he handed her the page, Jason felt her shiver again. "What is it, Yvette? There's something else. I can feel it."

She exhaled heavily. "Did you hear what he said when the other officer took him away?"

Smith had called out that he'd be back for her. The audacity.

Her serious blue eyes searched his. Seeking a comforting reassurance that Jason gave her without asking. It was easy, because he couldn't imagine being alone in this country, with no friends, and having been attacked.

"This town is small, but I take protecting the residents seriously," he said. "Do you want me to stay awhile?"

"No, I'll be fine. And you do need to take care of that man. Lock him up, will you?"

"That's my job. Just call me, okay?"

He headed to the door and pulled on his gloves. As he shoved his feet into his snow boots, he turned to look at her. She still sat on the couch, back to him, gaze focused out the tall windows that overlooked a snow-frosted birch forest not far behind the detached garage.

Was he doing the right thing? Leaving her here alone? The perp had been secured. But he couldn't know whether or not Smith had been acting alone. He'd make a point of checking in with her soon.

Jason couldn't shake the fact that there was a stranger staying in Frost Falls, and for some reason she had attracted danger to the small town. He believed that she didn't know Smith.

But what wasn't she telling him? What woman left for another country and only told her employer? Felt wrong. But he could attribute her nervousness to having just gone through a traumatic event. He'd give her some space.

"An hour," he said as he opened the door. "I want to hear from you!"

PULLING THE TRUCK along the side of the police station, Jason dialed up the radio volume just as the meteorologist announced everyone should head out for groceries. The blizzard was on its way and would be full force by tomorrow afternoon, possibly even the morning. He turned off the engine and got out with a jump. An inhale sucked in icy air. It was too cold for a storm, but the weather was always crazy in the wintertime.

Making a quick stop inside the station's ground level, Jason grabbed another krumkake from the plate on Marjorie's desk, then stepped right back outside. He swung around the building corner and opened the heavy steel back door. Down a short hall and then to the right, he clattered down the stairway that led to the basement cells. He hated this setup, especially when he had a drunk or violent perp to contain. More than a few times, he'd almost tumbled to the bottom with the prisoner in hand. Not the most well-designed police station, that was for sure.

The heater kept the cinder block–walled basement at a passable sixty-eight degrees and each of the three cells even held one of Marjorie's homemade quilts, along with a fluffy pillow. Jason had spent a night in one of the cells a few months earlier after a long night of reading over boring expense reports.

"We have a new guest in the Hotel Frosty?" he asked Alex and Ryan as he joined them before the middle cell.

"Just got him locked up. He's a fighter," Alex said. "Bay had to help me fingerprint him."

Jason noticed the black ink smear on Alex's jaw. "I see that. You get anything out of him, Bay?"

The man's focus was on his laptop again, set on a small table beneath a landline phone that hung on the wall opposite the cells.

"Not yet."

"All he's said," Alex added, "was a whole lot of words that were not favorable toward my mother."

"Is that so?"

Jason stepped up to the cell bars. Inside, the perp leaned against the back wall, one leg bent with his sole flat against the wall. Cowboy boots, not snow boots with traction on the soles. Idiot. The man lifted his chin. A position of challenge that didn't give Jason any more worry than if he'd spat at him.

"You are under arrest for assault," Jason stated. "James Smith, eh? I ran a trace on your plates earlier. You live in Duluth and work at Perkins. What's a line chef doing in Frost Falls strangling women?"

The man mumbled something and ended with two very clear swear words.

"He doesn't like your mother much, either," Alex said.

Jason smirked. "My mother would arm wrestle this skinny guy under the table if she heard him talking like that."

The Cash family—all three of the boys and both mother and father—was an athletically inclined bunch. Their father had been a marine before purchasing the Crooked Creek land and settling into dairy farming and to raise his family. And their mom, well, she was always trying new martial arts classes and once had flipped the eldest son, Justin, onto his back in an impressive move that had left their brother red-faced and Joe and Jason laughing like hyenas. Jason was never ashamed to admit it had been his mother who taught him some keen defense moves, including the more relaxed tai chi she practiced religiously.

The prisoner lifted his chin haughtily and then flipped them the bird.

"This is going to be a fun afternoon." Jason nodded to Ryan. "Why don't you get the paperwork started and bring down the DNA kit. You get mug shots?"

Alex blew out a breath and offered an unsure shrug. "Bay was taking the shots. Not sure."

"My camera was out of focus," Bay provided on a mumble. "I'm going through the shots right now. Might be one usable image."

"I get it," Jason said. "We'll mark this one down as uncooperative. Wait for fingerprints, then we'll check the CJRS." The Criminal Justice Reporting System was the US database for tracking and identifying criminals and those with police records.

"Will do, boss." Alex started up the stairs.

"And next time you come down, bring some of those krumkakes, will you?"

"If there's any left when I get through with them." Alex's chuckle was muffled by the closing of the upper door.

Jason turned, crossed his arms over his chest and couldn't help a smile. The man giving him the wonky eye might very well be a murderer.

"You interview the dead woman's friends?" Ryan asked as he joined Jason at his side.

"Haven't gotten that far yet."

"Storm's moving in. I hate Minnesota. I put in for a position in an Arizona county office."

"I'm sure they'll be happy to have you," Jason said. Bay was distracted, or probably didn't care much about the situation. Burnout? Maybe. Or it could be the weather. Damn cold was enough to make any man lose focus on what was most important.

And right now, Jason had added a beautiful Frenchwoman to that list.

"I should head out before it gets nasty outside," he said. "Ask this guy about girlfriends named Yvette. Or maybe it's his mom he's trying to strangle? Check the family stats on him."

"Will do," Bay said as Jason left him and headed out.

Chapter Seven

Amelie dialed the international number, and it went straight to her boss's voice mail. It was nearing midnight in France. Jacques needed to know about the attack on her, but, when fleeing France, she'd been instructed to keep any voice messages she left general and vague. He'd warned her not to communicate with him unless the situation were dire.

One man's definition of dire could very well be another man's idea of a challenge. It wasn't dire. She'd survived. Had the attacker intended to kill her? Rubbing her neck where his hands had clasped without mercy, she nodded. He would not have released pressure until she'd ceased breathing. But the police chief had arrived—the American expression was, in the nick of time.

So, not quite dire, but getting there.

Forgoing a message, she almost set down the phone, but then she remembered she'd told Jason she'd check in with him.

She dialed the number the police chief had written down for her. This call also went straight to message. She quickly relayed that she was fine and thanked him for his worry. Then without thinking, she added, "I owe you dinner at The Moose for your timely arrival to fight the bad guy. See you soon."

Dinner? Where had that come from?

She told herself that it made sense to befriend the chief of police—after all, she was alone here. It couldn't hurt to have an extra set of eyes watching out on her behalf, even if those eyes belonged to the most handsome man she'd seen in years.

"I'm just being practical," she said to the empty room.

Hanging up and tossing the phone onto the couch, she added, "Netflix and chill, indeed."

Wandering into the living room, she picked up a stray paper she'd not noticed earlier when cleaning up the mess from the struggle. It had slid partially under the couch. It was the beginning of her pros and cons list. One con read: *no love life.* Because working for an international police organization did tend to put a damper on relationships. Certainly, it was much easier when working in the tech department as opposed to having to go out in the field and never knowing where the job might take her. But still, it wasn't a job she could talk about with civilians. And that made getting close in a relationship difficult.

She set the paper on the desk, and as she did,

the lights flickered but did not go out. She suspected the electrical wiring for this old cabin was doing the best it could, given the harsh weather conditions. The rental owners had left instructions on how to use the generator, which sat outside hugging the east wall. As well, candles were in abundance, tucked in drawers, on windowsills, and placed in a box on the fireplace mantel.

Taking the lighter from the hearth, she lit the three fat candles fit into a birch log on the rustic wood coffee table. The ambience was nice, but the flickering flames didn't erase her lingering unease.

She rubbed her palms up and down her arms. She wasn't afraid. Not a damsel. But the question was: Was she safe here? Had someone found her because of what was in her head? What *was* in her head? She'd read a document on the computer. It had only showed up on the screen for ten minutes, and then it had disappeared. She had it all stored in her brain. And someone—her boss—had suspected what she'd seen could be dangerous.

The attack hadn't been random—someone seeking an easy victim in a desolate cabin far from town. He'd known her name. And in further proof, as the officers were dragging him out to the waiting vehicle, the attacker had said something about coming back for her.

An impossible task if he was in jail. But had he acted alone?

It wasn't uncommon for Interpol agents to go dark, especially when they were deep undercover. She wasn't exactly deep undercover, but Jacques had been adamant about keeping her off the grid. She may not have been out on assignment, but the extensive information lodged in her head made her dangerous, whether she liked it or not. She'd always trusted Jacques before. She'd continue to trust him now.

"Another week," she muttered. "That's all I'll give him before I reassess and change tactics."

"YOU LISTEN TO your messages?" Marjorie asked as she popped her head into Jason's office to say goodbye for the evening.

Jason had left Ryan Bay below to interrogate the prisoner, while he was still on his way out to question the other women who had been with Yvette Pearson on Saturday night at The Moose. He hadn't even glanced to his phone yet.

"Will do," he absently replied to Marjorie, his focus on the computer screen. James Smith did not have any known relatives listed.

"Uh-huh." Not convinced at all. "How's the prisoner?"

"Think he's from Texas. But we can't have a decent conversation with him that isn't three-quarters expletives."

"How's Ryan doing with him?"

"Guy's lackadaisical. He feels like one of those

mosquitoes that a guy always has to brush away, but the bug never gets too close to bite."

"Annoying?" Marjorie asked.

"That's the word."

"You taking the night shift to keep an eye on him?"

"No, Alex has the night shift. I'll come in early to relieve him. Unless the storm arrives. Then I might have to go for a ride."

"I know you're excited for the fresh snow." Marjorie chuckled. "You need to start racing, Cash."

"I would love to, but can't afford to take time off now. This is a big case."

"That it is. And I trust you'll handle it well."

"You've never seen what I can do with homicide. How can you be so sure, Marjorie?"

"Because you're smart and not about to take crap from anyone. Especially a man behind bars who may have murdered an innocent woman."

"Thanks for the vote of confidence."

"Yes, well, I see how you sometimes doubt yourself, Chief Cash."

He raised an eyebrow at that statement.

"You put yourself out there like the got-it-all-together, cocky police chief. And that's well and fine. You do have it all together. More than most of us do. But I know you were hurt by something right before you came here."

He'd never told Marjorie everything about his

reason for taking the job at the station, only that he had come fresh from the CIA.

"You're doing a good job, Cash," she said. "Don't ever forget that."

He nodded, finding it hard to summon a response. He tried his best with what he'd been given. And now he'd been handed a homicide investigation. How he handled this would prove to all watching him that he was capable and trustworthy.

He winked at her. "See you tomorrow, Marjorie," Jason said. "Tell Hank hey from me."

She waved and closed his office door.

Jason returned his attention to the police database. Along with the fingerprints, he entered a description, possible alias of James Smith, nationality and crime. Smith was not his real name. Well, it could be, but a search for "James Smith" brought up far too many hits, none remotely similar in looks to the man sitting below. And none matched the Duluth address from the license, which meant the owner of the license might never have committed a crime and had reason to be booked and have his fingerprints on record.

And that meant that whoever sat in the cell below had stolen the license and the vehicle.

Jason sat back in his chair and flicked the plastic driver's license Alex had taken from the man's wallet. It was easy enough to fake a license, but to take the time to coordinate that match with vehicle registration? Had to be stolen. By force?

Tugging open his top drawer, he pulled out a magnifying glass and studied the microprint on the license. The virtual image of the state bird— the loon—appeared to float and then sink on the card's surface as he viewed it from different angles. A rub over the surface felt like all the other licenses he'd held over the years. The card was not flimsy, either. The photo showed a nondescript man in his midthirties with brown hair and eyes who wore a green collared polo shirt. He looked like the man in the cell below, but—well, hell, anything was possible.

The SUV hadn't been listed as stolen when he'd run the check earlier. But if the original owner had been harmed in some way—or even murdered— the car may not yet have been reported stolen.

He picked up the phone and then called out to Marjorie, "You still here?"

"What do you need?"

Jason smiled. It always took her a bit to gather her things, and shut down the computer, and do a bit of dusting before she felt able to leave the office. "Will you patch me in to the Duluth desk?"

When the call was transferred, he gave the officer the VIN and the license info. There were no reports of theft.

"Will you drive out and check on James Smith?" Jason asked the officer. "I've got a perp here with his license and his vehicle, but I don't think he is who he wants us to believe."

"Will do. Give me an hour."

"Thanks." Jason hung up.

Time to head for Lisa Powell's place. He'd wanted to go sooner, but one of the drawbacks of being on a police force of two was that he had to do almost all of the work himself, from questioning to data search to writing reports. And Bay wasn't as helpful as he needed him to be. Fortunately, Powell lived down the block from him with her husband and a couple of kids. She had to know that Yvette Pearson was dead, but just in case, he'd proceed carefully. Being a Sunday, the whole family would be home. This was not going to be easy, but he did enjoy the interrogative procedure and modulating it for a nonaggressive subject.

Pulling out his phone, he spied the voice mail waiting for him. From Yvette. He hadn't forgotten about asking her to check in with him. She reported she was fine and…

"Dinner?" Jason nodded appreciatively. "Perfect opportunity to figure out who the hell Yvette LaSalle is."

Because in a short time, there had been a murder and then an attack on another woman. Coincidence? He didn't think so.

Chapter Eight

Both Lisa Powell and Hannah Lindsey had been upset to hear about Yvette Pearson's death. Both had known her from Blaine High School, where they'd graduated three years earlier. They, along with Hannah's mother, had been celebrating Lisa's birthday and had far too much to drink. Lisa had been inconsolable, so Jason had left her to her husband. Hannah had been in tears as well, but she'd said that Yvette had left The Moose to head back to the Snow Lake motel where she was staying. When he'd asked why they'd let their drunk friend drive, Hannah had broken out in a bawling fit.

Neither had mentioned a strange man watching them while they'd been partying in the back of The Moose. But would they even remember if they'd been that wasted? Yvette Pearson had gotten a ride to The Moose from Lisa, and yet no one in the Powell family had noticed the maroon Monte Carlo—Yvette's car—still parked out behind their garage in the alleyway until Jason had arrived. Yvette hadn't made the short four-block walk from The Moose to her car. Smith—if he were indeed the murderer—had to have offered her a ride. Very possibly, he'd ended her life somewhere in town.

That would have been an aggressive move on Smith's part. Not taking her to a private place to do the deed. It indicated he'd simply wanted her dead, and quickly. And he hadn't driven far to dispose of the body. Another indication of a rushed job.

Had he known Yvette Pearson? Had anger over something pushed him to take her life? Had she known him from Blaine? Did they work together? They might have known one another and he followed her here and waited until she was alone so he could strike. A crime of passion.

Except that those sorts of crimes were messier, more involved, and didn't involve the perpetrator going after yet another woman with the same name.

Unless, of course, an Yvette had hurt him in some way and he was taking out his anger on any random Yvette he stumbled upon?

Very possible. And the two women did bear a resemblance, both young and beautiful with long dark hair.

Now that Jason had spoken to the friends, he could go back to the office and, along with Bay, figure out a new interrogation strategy. Pearson's family would need to be interviewed, as well as those she worked with.

But really? If Elaine's final report showed Smith's DNA taken from under Pearson's fingernails, then the interrogation wasn't necessary. And the suspect had yet to ask for a lawyer. A good time stall on Jason's part.

He'd had the Monte Carlo towed to the station so Alex could give it a thorough once-over. And Marjorie would type up his audio notes from the interviews with the women in the morning.

Before it got too late, now was a good time to check in on Yvette. And maybe delve deeper into what the hell was happening in Frost Falls.

"WHY DO I suspect ulterior motives?" Yvette asked as he stepped inside the cabin.

"Just a routine check to ensure you're safe." Jason had handed her a heat-safe sack of food from The Moose. She *had* suggested dinner. "The meat loaf might need warming," he offered. "It's my favorite."

"I'm not sure I've had loaf of meat before," Yvette teased.

After he'd peeled away all his outer gear layers, Jason settled before the table as Yvette dished up warm meat loaf, mashed potatoes and the soft, buttered dinner rolls The Moose's owner made from scratch. Now this would hit the spot. She bustled about the kitchen while he attacked the meat loaf.

She'd seemed distant since the attack, and instinctively, he wanted to allow her space. But professionally? He could dig for a few relevant clues while engaging in casual conversation.

"I'm surprised a woman who seems prickly about our winter chose to vacation in Minnesota."

Yvette sat across the table from him and tore her bread roll in half. "The trip was a gift," she said. But he knew, from her inability to meet his gaze, that she wasn't being truthful. Not completely. "A friend of a friend knew the owner of this cabin. I thought I'd give it a try. And with the photography opportunities...like I've said."

"Fair enough." Using a quarter of the roll, Jason sopped up the butter melted in the concave top of his mashed potatoes. "I thought you said you trust me, Yvette?"

"I do."

"Then why are you lying to me?"

She pressed her fingers to her chest and gaped at him. Those blue eyes were hard to accuse, so he tried not to look into them for too long. But, man, what about those lush lashes? A guy could get caught in them and never wish to escape.

"You would never in a million years choose to vacation here," he said. "Or maybe it started out as a spur-of-the-moment trip, but I sense things have changed for you. You know why that man was after you, don't you?"

"I honestly don't. Swear to you that I don't. You can even give me a lie detector test if you need to." She bowed her head and poked at the mashed potatoes.

That was an odd defense. Bringing up the lie detector suggestion was something only those who were deeply worried being caught out with their lies would suggest. Was she shaking? Sure, there was a draft sitting here by the window, but he sensed she was not comfortable. And it wasn't because this could be misconstrued as a first date. It wasn't. But he sensed a little of that "get to know you but I'm nervous" vibe about her.

"Can you give me the name of the friend of a friend who suggested you vacation here?" he asked.

Now she looked at him straight on. And he didn't sense any shyness in that gaze. "You're investigating me now?"

"No, just trying to gather as many useful details as I can. You're a stranger to our town, and you've been targeted. I need to put together possible connections."

"I don't have the friend's name. I took the offer as a means to fill out my photography portfolio. I've always wanted to turn nature photography into a career. And I've never taken snowy shots. It was an opportunity, so I grabbed it."

Jason sat back. "Fine. But if I look you up in the international database, what will I learn?"

She shrugged. "That I live in Lyon, France. I have a job, rent an apartment, drive a Mini Cooper and—what else do those things reveal?—I've no police record. I've been hired for a few nature photography assignments for small publications over the last year."

"Kind of vague."

"Chief Cash, I'm not the criminal here. And I'm a bit offended that you're treating me like one."

"I'm offended that you don't want to help my investigation. Anyone with nothing to hide should be happy to help. The man could have killed you, Yvette."

"I know that." She took a sip of water and closed her eyes, looking aside.

Had he pushed too hard? Admittedly, Jason had never ranked high on the compassion stuff. Comforting victims after a crime was always a challenge for him.

Jason placed a hand over hers, and she flinched but then settled and allowed him to keep his hand there. "I've not had a case like this in…" She didn't need to know he was desperate to prove himself. "I've never had a homicide. Small town, you know? I just want to do things right. But if I've offended you, I'm sorry. It's hard for me to keep business separate from other things in this situation."

"Other things?" She lifted a brow.

Hell, he'd gone and said something he probably shouldn't have. And yet, if he couldn't be honest with her, then she had no reason to reciprocate. "I like you, Yvette. I feel protective toward you, and not just because it's my job to keep you safe."

Her nervous smile was too brief. "I like you, too, Jason Cash. I wish we could have met under different circumstances."

"Doesn't mean things can't go how we want them to."

"No, it doesn't." Now the smile returned, more confident.

"But I promise you," he said, making a point of meeting her gaze, "if I ever want you to have pie, it will be delivered in person, and shared."

"Makes sense. Now. It was a stupid thing to open that door. I should have been more suspicious."

Jason lifted his chin. "You have a reason to be suspicious?"

She shrugged. "Shouldn't any woman staying alone in a cabin in the middle of nowhere be cautious?"

He nodded, but again, his Spidey senses tingled. There was something she wasn't telling him.

The phone in Jason's pocket jangled. He reluctantly pulled his hand from Yvette's and checked the message. It was from Ryan Bay. He'd gotten a fingerprint hit on their prisoner. It was not a match to James Smith, line chef at the Duluth Perkins.

"I need to head in to the station," he said to Yvette.

"The investigation?"

"Yes. Sorry." He stood. "I hate to eat and run. And to leave things…well…"

She took his hand and squeezed it. "You know where to find me. Go. Do your job. Text me later if you can."

"That I will."

He almost leaned forward, but then Jason realized it would be for a kiss and—it didn't feel quite right. She'd been angry with him for the way he'd gone about asking her questions—a bit too angry for someone with nothing to hide. And he wasn't even sure what he wanted right now. To interrogate her or to romance her? Best to dial down the need for tasting her lips that he got every time he looked at those lush ruby reds. He had a job to do. He didn't need distractions.

Damn. Why did those blue eyes have to be so stunning? They possessed powers. He could feel them weakening his resolve as well as his legs. If he didn't move now, he'd sit and stay for a while.

Jason moved to the door and got dressed, backing out the front door with a silly wave as he did so. When he stood out on the snowy stoop and the chill clenched in his lungs, only then did he blow out a breath and shake his head.

"What's she doing to your head, man?"

RYAN FLAGGED DOWN Jason as he was driving toward his house. He pulled over and rolled down the truck window. Ryan leaned out the window of his white SUV. "I'm headed to Marjorie's house for supper. Wasn't sure when you'd be back, but I left the perp's outstanding arrests report on your desk."

"You got a digital file?" Jason asked.

"Sure. I can text it to you now." The man punched a few buttons on his phone, and a minute later Jason's phone rang with a message. "Perp's got some deep stats. Connects him to the Minnesota mafia."

Jason lifted a brow. The Minnesota mafia wasn't an official term; it was what those in the know used because it was easier to say than "the group of half a dozen families who joined with the infamous Duluth gang, the MG12, and were involved all over the state in everything from theft to money laundering, gun running and human trafficking."

And Jason had one of their ilk in his jail?

"I'm going to read up on them after I eat. Apparently Marjorie's husband, Hank, makes a mean roast beef and dumplings," Bay offered, as he was already starting to roll up his window. "It's cold out here! Stay warm, Cash!"

And with that, the man headed south toward the dispatcher's house. Hank did have a talent—Jason never passed up an invite for dumplings.

Now he could only sit there in the idling truck, window still down and cold air gushing in, as he scrolled through the report.

"I'll be," he muttered after he'd read it all. "Mafia. Really?"

The report named their James Smith as one Herve Charley, a Texas native who had no current known residence. Last three reports connected him to the Minnesota mafia. As a hit man. He specialized in close elimination, meaning he preferred to use his hands and not a weapon.

Jason swore. Yvette had managed to avoid harm from a hit man? Possibly the very same hit man who had taken out Yvette Pearson, a woman who bore a striking resemblance to Yvette LaSalle. What the hell was going on?

The last time he'd been in such proximity to a woman capable of handling her own against a dangerous predator had been in Italy, two years earlier…

Jason lay on the rooftop, peering through the sight of the .338 Lapua sniper rifle. He could hit a target a mile away with ease. Today the target was closer, less than a third of a mile in range.

He'd tracked the suspect's movements from the Accademia hotel down the street.

He made a minute adjustment to the rear sight. In forty seconds he would be in position for a kill shot.

It was a windless day, and fluffy off-white clouds dampened the sun. A bird chirped from a nearby tin flue that capped an air vent jutting up from the roof tiles. Perfect conditions to make the shot.

Behind him on the roof he heard Charleze click off on a phone call and say something to him. He ignored her. He was in the zone. No interruptions. She should know better. Thirty-five seconds...

"Jason?"

She had to know he could not chat with her now.

"It's off," she said.

He heard that. He didn't want to hear it. But he processed those two words and grimaced. Twenty-eight seconds...

"Jason Cash, did you hear me? Interpol wants the suspect alive."

Not according to his orders from the CIA. And he didn't answer to anyone but the Central Intelligence Agency. Charleze may have been his liaison here in Verona, Italy, helping him to navigate the ins and outs of this foreign land, but she was not his boss. And she didn't call the shots. Unless they were in bed. And...that had happened, too.

Sixteen seconds. He wouldn't increase pressure on the trigger until the eight-second mark. And he always shot on empty lungs. He began the exhale. The increase in oxygen to his eyes would help his visual acuity.

"Jason." *Her hand slapped over his trigger hand.*

The suspect wobbled out of sight. Jason lost the mark. He reacted, gripping Charleze by the shirt and pulling her down, nose to nose with him. "Do you know what you've done?"

"We want him alive," *she repeated succinctly.*

He squeezed the shirt fabric and shook his head. "We? Who we? The target wasn't yours to have. My orders were to take him out. And now you've spoiled that."

He rolled to his back, knowing he could set up and take another shot, but not without causing a commotion on the ground. He'd chosen the perfect kill shot, a place where the suspect would fall next to a brick building, out of the public's view.

Had she known that all along? Had she been stringing him along? Using him to get to the target?

He hated her for that. Wanted to grip her by the shoulders and force the truth out of her. But he couldn't do that until he got the full story from both his boss and hers.

"You're a sore loser," *Charleze suddenly said. She stood straight, looming over his prone posi-*

tion on the rooftop. The floaty white pants she wore listed against his forearm. The touch was mutinously soft. "He's one of our own, Cash. The FSB wants him alive to prosecute for crimes in our own country."

"Your own? The FSB is Russian federal security. You're with Interpol."

"Most of the time." Had red lips ever smiled with such evil relish? "I do enjoy this vacation in Italy. A breath of fresh air, if you ask me. Not to mention the sex with an American agent."

A double agent? Jason blew out a heavy breath. She was a honeypot. "You cost me the hit. He's killed dozens in the US. The CIA had jurisdiction on this case."

"If that's how you want to play it. I've done my job of babysitting you. Ciao!"

She turned on her sexy red heels and strutted across the rooftop to the door, walking inside and closing it behind her.

Babysitting him?

Jason turned to his side and swore.

He'd been played. She'd used him to track the target. She'd probably been relaying his position to her team while he'd been lining up the shot. Idiot! How had he allowed this to happen?

Because he'd slept with her and had let some long blond hair and pouty red lips sway his better judgment.

His boss would have his ass for screwing up

this one. Rightfully so. The target had been on a most-wanted list. His death had been imperative.

Now Jason pounded a fist on the steering wheel as he still sat idling on Main Street. He'd never run after Charleze. He'd lain there on the rooftop, stunned, his blood draining from his extremities as he'd processed the shock of it all. He should have gone after her. Should have...

Would have...

Could have...

There hadn't been a thing he could have done to change the outcome after he'd missed the shot. He'd known that then; he knew that now. And he had been punished for that screwup. But he'd always tried not to look at his employment in Frost Falls as punishment but rather, a new opportunity. And it had grown into a job he could be proud of. He loved the people who lived here. Sure, he wished for more real police work. Procedural stuff like the homicide he currently had on his docket. But what else to expect in a small town?

And now they would take that away from him, too.

Chapter Nine

The next morning, Jason hopped out of his truck behind the station house and closed the door. The patrol car, which Alex drove, was parked next to his.

The wind whipped at his face, and he smiled. Despite the ghosts of CIA past that had threatened to haunt him, he'd woken bright and shiny this morning, singing in the shower, and after re-reading the report on Charley, happier than a clam that he had him behind bars. He'd nabbed a mafia hit man. That should prove to those who had the inclination to keep an eye on him that he was worthy of a second chance. He seriously wanted to maintain his position as chief of police here in Frost Falls. It was small potatoes, sure, but it was a job he'd made his own.

He'd dressed quickly and headed for the station. The storm had arrived early. He looked forward to it, because in its wake the forecasted two to three feet of snow would invite him to plow through it going well over one hundred on the snowmobile. If he had a clear, open road to race along, he'd push the machine beyond 150 miles per hour. Grippin' it and rippin' it!

His phone jingled with the second reminder tone that played ten minutes after an initial message. Must have missed the first one. Pulling it out from inside his coat, he read the one-word text: Hurry! It was from Alex.

Jason crossed the lot in a race and pulled open the basement door. He called down to the cells, "Alex?"

He descended the stairs quickly. Half a bloody footprint stamped the bottom step. And there before an open cell door lay Alex, sprawled on the floor. His face bled, and he was out cold. His fingers were still wrapped about his cell phone. No sign of the prisoner.

Jason lunged to the floor and shook the officer.

The man roused and groaned, touching what Jason figured was likely a broken nose. It was then Jason noticed the bruise marks about his neck.

Alex coughed and gripped his throat. "Sorry, Cash. I had to open the cell to push in the food. The Moose packaged it up in a box and bag, and I didn't have a plate to slide through the meal slot, so…"

"It's all right, Alex. He tried to choke you?"

Alex nodded. "He was strong. Think I saw my life flash before my eyes. I can't believe I let him get the better of me."

"That's a pattern," Jason said.

"What?"

Jason tapped Alex's throat where the skin was already turning deep purple. "The girl in the ditch. Yvette LaSalle was almost strangled. And now you. They're all connected. Have to be."

"Last night... I asked him how long he'd been in town." Alex gasped and winced, touching his nose tenderly. "You know, trying to tease out more information from him."

"And?"

Alex clutched Jason's sleeve. "He said...since Saturday morning."

"Really?"

"Yes, and then I asked if he'd visited The Moose that night, and he grinned like the Joker. I could feel his evil slide over my skin like some kind of nasty weeds at the bottom of a lake. Creepy."

"He was there," Jason guessed. "I bet he was watching Yvette Pearson, then he followed her."

Wincing and easing his fingers over his neck, Alex asked, "How long have I been out?"

"The text rang through ten minutes ago. I only just noticed it. I gotta get out there now. Pick up his trail. I'll call Marjorie and have her come over to fix you up!"

Dialing Yvette's number while he stomped up the stairs, out around the side of the building and into the station, Jason swore when his call went to messages. He left a quick one: Lock your doors. Don't answer any knocks unless it's me.

He shoved the phone in his pocket, realizing that had been cryptic and would freak out a person. He'd not take more than a few minutes here before heading out to pick up the suspect's trail. He dialed Marjorie and told her he'd found Alex in bad shape. She could be over in less than five minutes, because she was pulling out her laundry at Olson's Oasis.

A few minutes later, Marjorie stomped into the station house and set a laundry basket aside on the floor.

"Marjorie, I need you to put out an APB on the suspect Herve Charley. Using the false name James Smith. Put it out across the Boundary Waters, St. Louis County and the rest of the state. The BCA hasn't reported in yet this morning. Give Bay a call and ring Robert Lane to come in and give us backup."

The county frequently spread their law enforcement employees from town to town when help was needed. Small towns like Frost Falls generally never required more than two at any given time. But Jason had a potential murderer on the loose, and with Alex injured, he couldn't do this himself. Nor would he want to risk screwing up the case because he was too proud to ask for help.

"Check your messages!" Marjorie said as he paced his office.

"Will do. I'm heading out to take a quick run through town, but—" He knew the suspect could only be moving in one direction. "On second thought, I'm headed for the Birch Bower cabin to check on Yvette."

"The dead woman?"

"No, Miss LaSalle. The French chick renting the Birch Bower cabin."

"Oh, right. He attacked her yesterday."

"And he might be going back for a second attempt."

"Take the four-by-four with the snow chains on the wheels," Marjorie offered.

"Nope. The cat will get me there faster, and if the snow drifts, I'll have to dig the truck out. Won't have to do that with the snowmobile."

Marjorie sighed. "Fine. But take one minute to listen to your messages before you leave. There's a weird one on there from Interpol asking about Emily."

"Emily?"

"Something like that. Just listen to it."

Jason eyed the blinking red light on the desk phone, indicating he had a message. She had told him to listen to his messages yesterday, but he'd gotten distracted. A weird one?

He pushed the button on the phone and listened to the male voice, which had a French accent similar to Yvette's.

"I am Jacques Patron, assistant director with

Interpol in Lyon, France. This is urgent. My employee Amelie Desauliniers is staying in your town. I've been unable to reach her. She is in danger. You must —"

A crash sounded in the background on the phone line. Jason gripped the edge of the desk.

"Protect her!" shouted over the phone.

The next sound was too familiar to Jason. A gun fired. And then an abrupt shuffle was followed by static.

Had the caller just been shot? Not *just*. This message had been on his phone for over a day. Jason winced. What the hell?

Jason called out, "Marjorie, when you're finished nursing Alex, I need you to trace the call that was on my messages. I think it's recorded another murder."

"*Uff da*, are you serious? I thought it sounded odd. And who is Emily?"

"Amelie. And I don't know."

Jason rubbed his jaw. This new development only added to the mystery. He needed to call Interpol, verify that the caller was indeed who he said he was and then find out if he were dead or alive. He'd asked about Amelie? An employee of his.

He had a foreign spy hiding out in Frost Falls?

And there was a strange Frenchwoman staying out at the Birch Bower cabin who seemed oddly capable of defending herself and yet protective of personal details.

Could Yvette LaSalle be undercover? Using a different name? Or was there another French-woman hiding out in the town?

"I have to get out there." Jason checked the Glock holstered at his hip with a clasp over the solid shape, then zipped up his coat. "Sorry you had to come in when you should be home with Hank preparing to ride out the storm. Call me when you've got a trace on that call. And...have Bay call Interpol and verify a Jacques Patron is assistant director."

"Sure thing, boss." She bent to scribble that information on a piece of paper. "You check in with me once you're out at the Birch Bower place. I don't want to learn you've gotten stuck in a snow-bank."

"You know I'm smarter than that!" Jason pulled the door shut behind him. The wind blasted him so fiercely, he took a step back to counter his sudden loss of balance.

Straddling the snowmobile, he fired it up. Pulling on the helmet stopped the pricks of icy snow crystals from lashing at his eyes and face. The storm had picked up. Soon enough, the winds would be vertical. The music blasted inside his helmet, and he turned it off. He wanted to hear when he got a call from dispatch.

Or if he got a plea-for-help call from Yvette.

Pulling up to the gas station, Jason ran out and into the store. He'd had the SUV towed after Alex had given it a once-over, finding no evidence. It was in a Duluth impound lot by now. And of course, it was stolen, belonging to a man he'd yet to learn was safe or even alive.

"Any new rentals this morning, Rusty?"

The old man shook his head. He had a coat on and keys in hand. He stood up straighter at the sight of Jason's urgency. "What's up, Cash?"

"Just following a lead."

"Did that foreigner take off with my rental?"

"If you consider Texas foreign, I suppose so. I found it out near the Birch Bower cabin. It's been impounded as evidence."

"Ah, shoot."

"Don't worry. You'll have it back in a month. You haven't seen that man in the last half hour, have you? Looking for another rental? Walking the streets?"

"Nope, and I pay close attention to what's going on in this little town. You know all I have to do during the day is sit and stare out at everything."

"I do know that. But you're headed home now?"

"No one needs gasoline during a storm."

"And if they do, they can help themselves," Jason said of the station owner's generosity at allowing customers to pay him the next day if they ever needed a fill-up at odd hours. "Give me a ring if you see him on your way home. Deal?"

Rusty nodded. "Sounds like you've got something exciting going on."

"Nothing I can't handle. Talk to you later, Rusty."

Jason got back on his snowmobile and turned on the ignition. Smith, aka Herve Charley, could have fled town. But without killing his target? Didn't sound like a reliable hit man. He must be lying low. That's what Jason would do if he were in the man's shoes.

That message from Jacques Patron bugged the hell out of him. It almost felt...staged. But he'd heard the gunshot. Or had he?

Jason tugged out his cell phone. Bay would have contacts in the FBI. They might be able to get more from Interpol, and quicker, than a simple small-town police chief.

THE WIND WHIPPED blinding snow through the open cabin door as Amelie welcomed Jason Cash inside. He stomped his boots and slapped his gloved hands together. That was followed by a short jump, which successfully released most of the snow from his head, shoulders and boots to the door mat.

Closing the door behind him, he offered her a rosy-cheeked smile, but concern flickered in his green eyes. "You okay?"

"Yes. Two visits in as many days. A girl could only get so lucky." And maybe she'd been wrong earlier to think he was suspicious of her. "Why did you brave the storm to come out here?"

"Didn't you get my message?"

"No, my phone is dead. Was just going to charge it when you knocked on the door. The electricity keeps flickering on and off. I suspect it'll be a cold, dark day." She noticed his tense jaw. "What's going on, Jason? Now you're frightening me."

"Sorry, didn't mean to. You're safe. That's what matters." He glanced out the window, where only a sheet of white could be seen. "Visibility on the main roads is already less than zero, but if a guy knows where he's headed, he can make it a few miles out here. As for the electricity, you're probably right to suspect it could cut out on you. You should start a fire in the hearth."

"I'd love to, but the wood out back is frozen. I was going to head out with an ax, but it's not that difficult for a girl to talk herself out of hard labor."

He seemed like he had something else to say, but he only clenched his jaw. "I'll bring in some wood," he said after a moment. "Safety precautions first." He slapped his palms together. "I'll head around back and—where's the back door?"

She pointed across the living room.

"I'll bring the wood to that door. Uh…you might want to gather some candles and check if there's a radio as well. With predicted snowfall of twenty-four inches, you're going to get snowed in for sure," he said as he stomped across the living room to the back exit.

He left, slamming the door shut, which whisked

in a mist of icy crystals that shivered across Amelie's face. The wind howled and whipped wickedly outside. She could barely make out the man's silhouette as he walked by the back window. His black snow gear was obliterated by the whisks of wind and snow. Kind of him to bring in some wood. And much appreciated.

He had been worried about her? That went beyond nice. That was plain sweet. But also, a policeman doing his job. She'd been attacked. She appreciated having a hearty, handsome man show up when she felt most vulnerable.

Back in the kitchen, Amelie plugged her cell phone in to recharge. With hope, there could be a message on it from Jacques Patron.

Chapter Ten

Amelie met Jason at the back door after he'd made four trips and had deposited some surprisingly dry logs in the iron fire dogs designed to hold half a cord of wood. It was already growing dark outside, and with the visibility so low, the sky was fuggy and gray.

Now he pulled off his outer gear and she hung his hat, gloves and scarf on a hook by the front door. He'd brought in a palpable chill, but it was tinged with his cologne, which was a mix of pine and spice. Maybe it was his natural scent? She could breathe him in all day.

"I've water on the stove for hot chocolate, then I'll start the fire," she said.

"You take care of the treats. I got the fire situation under control. Looks like there's some of those handy fire starters on the mantel." He crossed the room and placed a few logs in the hearth.

Checking that the water wasn't yet boiling, Amelie glanced at her phone, charging on the little stand next to the toaster. "You said you'd left me a message?"

"No need to check it," he called from before the fireplace. He knelt, clicking the lighter until the starter he held took to flame. He nestled it within the logs, holding it there until the wood started to smolder. When satisfied he'd gotten a flame going, he stood. "I called because…"

She wandered over, gesturing he take a seat on the couch while they waited for their respective projects to heat up.

Jason settled onto the old yellow-and-green-checked couch and sighed. "The prisoner escaped. Tried to strangle Alex when he was serving him breakfast and took off. That's why I headed out here. To make sure you were safe. After cruising around town and not finding any trace of him, I suspect the guy has holed up somewhere. That's a good thing. Maybe. He could be inactive until the storm passes."

"He tried to strangle an officer?" Amelie clamped her fingers about her neck. She had faint bruises from the attack, which was why she'd put on a turtleneck this morning. "You think I'm in danger? Again?"

"The man's on the loose, Yvette. You were lucky that I arrived in time yesterday."

She nodded and glanced to the desk where she'd been writing out her pros and cons. Another con? Being pursued by a relentless killer.

A log in the fireplace snapped and took to a glowing yellow blaze. The heat wasn't yet palpable, and the cozy scene didn't settle her nerves. Amelie pulled a blanket folded over the back of the couch about her shoulders.

"If he was intent on harming you, or ending your life, I have to believe he won't leave until the job is done." Jason glanced to her. "Sorry. Shouldn't have said it like that. But I won't lie to you."

"Of course not. I need to know the truth." She tugged the blanket tighter around her shoulders.

"And then there's the phone call from Interpol," Jason said.

She sat upright. She hadn't told him she worked for Interpol. Unless Jason had talked to Jacques Patron? Had the assistant director filled him in? Could she come clean to Jason?

The police chief tilted his head and eyed her fiercely. Amelie felt as though he were trying to read her, to look inside and divine her truth. Truths she had been trained to protect at all costs. He knew something. He must.

"Jacques Patron," he said. "From Interpol." He rubbed his hands together, blew into them, then shot her another delving look. It felt like a blade stabbing at her throat. "Are you a spy?"

"No!" And then she said more quietly, "Yes. I'm not sure. Maybe?"

Did the man have a thing about spies? He

wasn't making a point of being open-minded, at least not with his actions. Spies weren't all evil and double-crossing.

"Why would you guess at something like that?" she asked.

"Maybe? Seriously?" He rubbed his jaw with both palms. A sigh had never sounded more exasperated. "How can you not know if you're a spy? It's time you let me ask you some questions."

"What did Jacques tell you, exactly?"

He compressed his lips and nodded. "I get it. Not going to spill the details. Just like a spy."

"I'm not a spy, Jason. I mean…"

"Listen, Yvette—or is it Amelie?—this is serious. And I need your help. Before I met you in The Moose, I'd just come from a crime scene. Dead body of a young woman found in the ditch. Homicide. Ligature marks around her neck. She had long dark hair, and I'd place her at about your age. And…we got an ID on her. Her first name was Yvette."

"That's…"

"Not a crazy coincidence. We have more French Canadians up in our parts than in the lower region of Minnesota. If you're in the business, you know this is all tied together. Or you have to suspect as much."

"But that would mean—" Amelie swallowed. "The man who attacked me killed an innocent woman because he thought…she was me? What about her family? Oh my goodness."

"I don't normally divulge details of an ongoing investigation to citizens, but it seems like you are involved in some way. And the call from Interpol really threw me for a loop. What is going on? Is your name Yvette or Amelie?"

"I…" Jacques had used her real name. That was the only way the police chief could know such a thing. Unless he'd had her checked out—no. Yvette LaSalle, aspiring photographer, was a hastily created cover that only she and Jacques knew about.

"He specifically asked for Amelie?" she asked carefully.

"Yes. Amelie Des—something or other. He was speaking quickly. Listen, I know something is up with you. You haven't felt right to me since I met you in The Moose. If you're on some kind of a mission—"

"I'm not. I promise."

"Then why do I have a dead body sitting in the Duluth morgue? And an escaped strangler who may or may not be pursuing any woman named Yvette?"

Why, indeed. If someone had truly discovered she had been hiding out here in Minnesota, would they have actually gone after the wrong Yvette? That would make for a very inept hit man.

And yet, someone was after her. She couldn't ignore that fact.

An innocent woman had been murdered. And the killer was now on the loose. She could tell Jason some of her truth. She had to. "I'm no longer a field operative."

He lifted a brow.

"I was a field agent for Interpol for six months."

Jason nodded and clasped his hands before his nose. Thinking. Deciding whether he could trust her? He could. The question was, could she trust him?

"Why didn't Jacques call me?" she asked. "I've been waiting to hear from him."

"The message said he wasn't able to get in touch with you. Amelie. Is that your real name?"

She nodded. "That's strange. The burner phone Jacques gave me—" She stopped before it was too late.

But it already was.

"There's only one reason a person has need for a burner phone, Yvette. Amelie."

"Actually, there are many reasons for any person to want to keep a phone not connected to a network."

He gave her another look of exasperation.

"You're with law enforcement, Jason. You know I can't tell you things."

"If you were on an active case, I might accept that excuse. *Are* you on a case?"

She shook her head.

"But you're not telling me something because…? Do you know why that attacker was after you? Why he wanted you dead? And why would your boss call and beg me to protect you, the call ending in the sound of a gun firing?"

"A gun? What happened? Is Jacques all right? What's going on?"

"You tell me. All I know is the man pleaded with me to protect Amelie, who he said was an employee of his, and then I heard a gunshot and a struggle before the connection went staticky. Marjorie is tracing the call, but I'm going to guess you can give me a direct number."

"He's assistant director at the Lyon office of Interpol. Of course you can get that number. I tried to call Jacques on his personal line earlier, and it went to message. Again."

She caught her forehead against her palm and exhaled. Her world had just tilted. Again. And this time she wasn't sure how to right things herself. She had to tell Jason her story. It was the right thing to do. Especially if she wanted help from law enforcement.

"I am supposed to be dark," she said. "No contact. Wait for Jacques to call me. The last time I spoke to him was on the evening that I hopped a flight to the US. And now such a strange call to you." She stroked her throat and swallowed roughly. "I am in danger, Jason. For something I know."

"Yeah?" He lifted his chin. His gaze was not soft or reassuring. He wasn't willing to give her the benefit of the doubt. She didn't blame him for his caution. Certainly, she would be cautious in this situation. "And what is it you know, Yvette?"

"That's the problem. I have the information in my head, but I don't know what it means."

She exhaled, her shoulders dropping. In the two weeks she had been hiding out here in the States, she'd gone through a list of those people she trusted, who might help her, if she needed to reach out. That list had included only Jacques Patron. She had no close family. And her few friends were all clueless as to her real job.

If she was going to survive, she needed to give Jason as much information as she was able. And then hope that she could trust him.

"It's why I'm here. My boss sent me into hiding after I told him about a strange list I read. I work in information systems and technology. Data tech, for short. We receive coded documents and dossiers all the time. The information is sorted and filed. But the last email I took in was something I'd not seen before. I thought Jacques should know about it. I didn't print it out—there wasn't time to—but I had skimmed it as I was wondering what it was about. I went to his office to tell him."

"And?"

"He asked me to write it out for him, which I did. After he glanced at it, he expressed worry that what I had seen would attract danger to me. He immediately sent me home. Then, in the middle of the night, I got a call from him telling me to be at the airport in two hours. I grabbed my bug-out kit, was given a fake passport for Yvette La-Salle and hopped in a cab, headed to Lyon-Saint Exupéry airport, and…here I am. Still waiting."

Jason swiped a hand over his chin. "You know something but you don't know what it is?"

"Exactly."

"But you just said he asked you to write it out for him. You remembered the whole list you'd read on the computer screen? I don't get it."

"I have a photographic memory for certain instances, like when reading. I never forget a single sentence in any book I read. And documents and lists that I've read? I can recall them perfectly. Coded lists? I may not know what they mean, but I retain all the data like a computer. Even un-coded items may baffle me if I don't know the original context."

Amelie pressed her palms together before her lips and closed her eyes. Her worst nightmare was coming true. "Jason, I've got a list in my head, and someone wants to kill me for it."

Chapter Eleven

Amelie rushed into the kitchen to remove the boiling kettle from the stove. She busied herself with pouring water into mugs to make hot chocolate. But more so, she simply didn't want to face Jason's questions. Because he would have a lot. His gaping expression after she'd confessed what was going on had spoken volumes.

But she couldn't avoid those questions. No smart agent would withhold information that could help to solve a case.

Placing the mugs on a tray, she turned to find Jason standing right behind her. She hadn't heard him approach and was so startled she sucked in a breath. He steadied her hold on the tray as she felt it slip. His warm palm slipped over the back of her hand, and all her focus went to that touch.

"Sorry," he offered. "Didn't mean to pull a sneak on you."

Were his green eyes freckled with brown? Mercy. Why did he have to be such an attractive man?

"So what do I call you now? Amelie or Yvette?"

Just when she was getting used to the cover name... "Amelie is my name. But I wonder if keeping the cover name might be easier when we're around others."

He shook his head. "Woman, you are full of surprises today. Let me get this for you, Yvette." He pronounced it purposefully. "Smells great. I love hot chocolate." He carried the tray over to the couch.

While she pressed a palm over her thundering heart. Chocolate. Handsome man. Sneak charm attacks? A tantalizing touch? Nothing about this day was going to be easy.

Over on the couch, Jason patted the seat beside him. Mug in hand, he put up his feet, clothed in striped wool socks, on the coffee table and sipped.

"I don't know if I can do this with you being Mr. Casual," she blurted out.

He sat upright. "Sorry, thought I was making you comfortable. Making it easier to talk and tell me your deepest, darkest secrets."

"That's a covert tactic."

"You know that from experience?" His tone was still calm, but that question had been edged with a sharp interrogative skill.

"I'm not a spy, Chief Cash. Not anymore."

Amelie sat a few feet away from him on the couch and grabbed the other mug from the tray. It was too sweet, but it was warm, and she needed that right now. The heat from the fireplace didn't quite reach the couch, for the logs were still kindling to flame.

"Please, call me Jason. And I'll stick with Yvette, since I agree that would be wisest. For now."

"I'm good with that."

"And, uh…with the snow blowing like a banshee, I think I'm stuck here for a while, so I hope you don't mind me getting comfy. And asking you the hard questions."

Amelie nodded. "Snowed in with…" She thought, *a sexy cop*, but said "…the local law enforcement. I'm feeling very safe, indeed. As for the hard questions?"

Time to come clean. With hope, she'd gain an ally and not be put on his suspects list.

After a sip to fortify her courage, she started, "Like I said, I'm a data technician. For Interpol. I sit in an office and type reports and do field research. Of course, my field is bits and bytes. It's something I excelled at in college but had set aside for the excitement and adventure of being a field operative. Until that position no longer fit me. Anyway, I was learning to program and hack all sorts of electronic and digital devices from a distance."

"You a code breaker?"

"Not as accomplished at that skill as I'd like. But with more training, it could happen."

And was that what she wanted to happen? Her pros and cons list was weighted to one side. And no matter how many ways she found to list "using my intellect" and "keeping up with technology" as pros, the heaviest side remained the cons.

Jason cast her a quirk of brow and a gaze that said she wasn't going to get away with any lies. "And does what's up have to do with something related to an Interpol case? You said something about having information but not knowing what that was."

"Exactly. But I don't know if it's an active investigation. Is it covert? Need to know? What's going on in my absence? I haven't been informed beyond 'keep your head down and we'll call you.' I thought the document I viewed was random business details. It looked like an invoice. My boss didn't clarify anything about it."

"So less than twelve hours after you brought it to his attention, he asked you to assume a new identity, leave the country and...you just did?"

"I trust him."

"Why is that?"

Amelie narrowed her gaze on the man. Was he intimating something deeper existed between her and Jacques? There wasn't anything between them. Not that she hadn't had the occasional fantasy. The man wasn't married, but she knew he had a model girlfriend who liked to be treated as if a queen.

"Jacques Patron had been on the same training team as my father decades ago. My dad always had good things to say about Jacques. That he was kind and had the other guy's back. I've known Director Patron over the years, but only from answering phone calls to my parents, and once I met him at a holiday party. After my hire at Interpol, I immediately trusted him, simply knowing how much my father trusted him.

"Jacques was the one I went to when I realized I couldn't cut it in the field. He didn't judge. Instead, he helped to reassign me. And when he learned about my memory, he started using me for special assignments."

"Such as?"

"I can't tell you about them."

"Right. Need to know and all that secure state secrets stuff."

"Exactly. But I can explain how my brain works. My current position sees me sitting before the computer, sometimes mindlessly typing in lists or code, or whatever comes across my desk. I don't process it in the moment, but trust me, it all gets retained here." She tapped her skull. "My ability sounds weird to others, but I've known nothing else since childhood."

"Like a kid who has colorblindness?" Jason asked. "He never knows he sees the world differently until someone points it out to him?"

"Exactly. I retain it all. And yet, not all. It's

termed eidetic memory, or photographic memory. The eidetic term refers more to recalling memories like a photograph, and the photographic memory is more related to lists, text and detailed information. What is weird is that sometimes I'll get to the grocery store and realize I've forgotten what I'd gone there for. I don't remember short lists, appointments or even conversations. It's only long lists and random coded data that seem to lodge in my brain. Book text, as well. But if I could ever remember what day my yoga class was scheduled, my instructor would stop giving me the side eye when I wander in on the wrong day."

Jason smirked. "Yoga and covert operations. You're a very interesting woman."

She'd take the compliment, but only because she needed it right now. Anything to make her feel safe and accepted by the one man who could very well make her life miserable. Because if he wanted to, he could turn the tables and investigate her, insist she tell him the things she didn't dare reveal. Or force her.

Jason took another sip of the hot chocolate, then asked, "You've been in Minnesota how long?"

"Two weeks."

"Witness protection?"

"We call it going dark."

"So still working for Interpol, but for all intents you're on an extended vacation."

"Exactly. Let me explain from the beginning. I originally trained as a field operative."

"A spy." He hung his head, and his grimace was obvious.

"Yes, you can call me a spy." Because she did like the term. Something strangely romantic about it. "Former spy, that is. My parents both worked for their respective governments. My father was Interpol and my mother, well…"

Telling him that sad tale wouldn't be easy, and it wasn't necessary to this case. If she were to keep the tears to a minimum, all information about her mother had to stay in the past. Where it belonged.

"The desire to serve my country is in my blood," Amelie continued. "And I've told you about Jacques Patron, and how I grew up trusting him. But after a few months of fieldwork, it grew apparent to me that I would never be able to take another person's life if it became necessary. I couldn't do what I'd been trained to do. Sure, I can use martial arts to defend myself and fend off an attacker. Though I was a bit rusty yesterday. Anyway, I can track and follow, surveil, assess a dangerous situation, but…" Amelie bowed her head and exhaled. "I couldn't bring myself to pull the trigger at a moment when it was necessary to stop a suspect. I choked. Aiming at a human body is a lot different than shooting at targets and ballistic dummies."

"That it is," Jason agreed. "You didn't think,

during training, that your job might lead you to life-or-death situations?"

"Of course. But training and real-life experience are vastly different. It's hard to explain. And I'd been surrounded by other recruits eager to prove themselves. I fell into the tough-girl mien. But that has never been me. Or at least, I thought it *could* be me. You know, grow up and take after your parents. Show them you've got the same grit in your blood." She sighed heavily. "I learned differently."

"You handled the attack from Smith like a pro. Make that Herve Charley."

"That's the perp's real name? Where is he from? Did you get a rap sheet on him? Who is he?"

"I'm asking the questions here, remember? What I just told you is what I know so far. And you were telling me how a spy came to sit behind a desk typing in coded lists."

"Sorry, it's natural to want to know everything I can about the guy who tried to kill me."

"I'll grant you that. Go on."

"Fine. After I realized I couldn't pull the trigger, I went to Jacques Patron. They'd spent a lot of money training me. I was disappointed in myself. In an effort to maintain some dignity and save face, I blurted out that I had a photographic memory."

"That didn't come up in training?"

"It really is something innate to me. I don't

bring it up because…" She shrugged. "It's my normal. And the skill may have helped with maps and topography and following long, detailed instructions in training, but for the real world, action, think-on-your-feet stuff, it doesn't make much of a difference. But Patron was intrigued at my, as he termed it, 'superpower,' so he put away the dismissal form and assigned me to the tech department. He tested me with a few assignments. I'd receive a classified document that I was to memorize and then later repeat when it was needed. I call it parlor tricks. But Patron was impressed."

"Sounds a little underhanded to me, but go on."

She'd never call it underhanded, but there had been times Amelie had wondered if Jacques was using her for reasons that no one else in Interpol was aware. Sort of his secret data weapon. And she'd not questioned him. In fact, it had made her feel more useful, like a part of the team again.

"One day an unconfirmed email arrived in my box. All incoming documents go through a secure server and are verified with a four-point internal security check. No one can hack into the system. And hacking *out* is even harder. I initially thought it was a regular invoice that got misdirected. I see them once in a while. Agent reports. Expense summaries. Purchase orders. I forward them to Accounts. It didn't give me pause. Until I started reading the data. Dates, dollar amounts, locations. And that mysterious fourth column. I'd never gotten something like that delivered by email. I was going to transfer it to Accounts when I noticed the sender's email was untraceable. That put up an alert. And…for some reason, I read it. Just sat there and read each line. It only took ten minutes."

"You went against protocol?"

"Yes, and no. It hadn't specifically been assigned to me, but Jacques was aware I retain all the information I see. Because it was an odd thing, I knew I had to tell him about it. I called him, and when I was going to transfer the email to him, it blew up."

"Blew up?"

"It was on a timer. It had been set to destruct so many minutes after an open reference was received, and then it did the cyber version of self-destructing. The weird thing was, after I'd written out the list at his request, Jacques merely glanced at it and seemed to know what it was for. I mean, he didn't state that specifically—it was a feeling I got at the time. He suggested I resume work, not worry about it. But he called me twenty minutes later and told me to go home for the day."

"You didn't think that was strange?"

"A little, but he didn't sound upset. And, as I've said, I trust him. I knew whatever I had seen was out of the ordinary."

"The guy must have known it was sensitive information."

"He did, but he didn't tell me what it was. He burned the list I'd written for him."

"So he just burned it? Never to be seen again?"

"He knew that the information could be accessed anytime because it's always in my head, no matter if I write it out or not."

"You must have a crowd in your brain."

She smiled. "I sometimes wonder about that, and then I realize the reason I can't remember to pick up milk along with cereal at the grocery is because my brain is crammed with too much other stuff. Ninety percent of which means nothing to me."

"You sure you don't have some international secrets locked away up there?"

"Well." Amelie set down the mug and tucked her palms between her legs. She faced Jason on the couch. "It is always a possibility."

His lift of brow told her he was intrigued.

"That night," she continued, "Jacques called me at home. It was after midnight. He'd booked a flight for me that left in two hours. He'd also given me a new passport and a new identity. He said the data I had in my head was so sensitive he feared for my safety and that I needed to go into hiding for a few weeks."

Jason whistled. "You gotta love the international spy game. But you've been trained to bug out?"

"Of course. I had a bugout bag packed for such an occasion. It was scary, but at the same time, I've been trained to handle situations like that. I took a cab to the airport. Nine hours later I arrived in Minneapolis, then a car drove me four hours to…this strange land that reminds me half of the tundra and half of a bizarre movie I've seen where the bad guy gets stuffed in a wood chipper."

"I love that movie." Jason cleared his throat. "Ahem. You said you've been here two weeks."

Amelie sighed and nodded. "I'm waiting for the all's clear from my boss."

"The same boss who called me and…" He winced.

She had forgotten about that strange message he'd received. Ending with the sound of a gunshot? Was Jacques okay?

"It baffles me," Jason said, "if a professional was sent after you, that he could make such a stupid mistake. To kill the wrong person?"

"He had to have asked her name." Amelie worked it out. "Might have looked her up. Followed her."

"But then he would have had her last name and should have known she wasn't the right target. And she's from a suburb north of Minneapolis. Was visiting friends here in town. Was in The Moose Saturday night, partying."

"He tracked her from Minneapolis?"

"I don't think so. I'm guessing he knew to look for his target in Frost Falls and, well—he found the wrong Yvette. That woman was in the right place at the wrong time."

Amelie started to work it out. The only person who knew she'd been staying here as Yvette LaSalle was her boss, and now Jason. So if she had been targeted because of her assumed name...

"Is your boss the only one who knows you're here?" he asked.

She met his pointed gaze with a gape. "But Jacques would never..." No, she trusted him. He'd given her a second chance when he didn't have to. "On the other hand, someone purchased my plane ticket. Made arrangements for the car when I arrived here. Jacques can't be the only one aware of my location, or that I'm hiding under an assumed name. And you know the spy trade. If someone wants to find another, they will."

"True. But there's something I'm missing. If you can help me to understand what it is you know that someone would kill for, that would help."

"That's the thing. The only way I can learn what I have in my head is to write it out. It's how the memory process works. I can't jump into the middle of a list of data. I need to write it from beginning to end."

"You didn't think to write it out when you got here?"

She shrugged. "I've been settling in, adjusting to this cold place, and what good would it have done? I've looked at it before. I didn't know what it was then—why would I know now?"

"I'd like to take a look at it. I'll keep the fire

stoked if you will put your pen to paper. Are you willing to give it a go?"

She nodded.

"Sounds like a plan. I'll check in with Marjorie. See if she's gotten a trace on the call from your boss. I'm going to run out and park the snowmobile in your garage. With the way the wind is blowing, if I leave it out, the snow might drift over the top of it."

"Thank you, Chief—er, Jason. I know this is the last thing you want to do on a stormy day."

"Actually, this is what I most want to do. You're in danger? I want to protect you. It's my job. But also…" He winked. "I'd hate to see the prettiest woman in Frost Falls get harassed by a hired killer."

"Harassed?" Amelie laughed at that, only because it was so assuredly not what had happened to her. The man had meant business. She was lucky to be alive.

"I know." He stood. "But I'm trying to not be so direct."

"Please. Be direct. I'm a big girl. I can handle the truth. You want to protect me from someone who has me on his hit list? I'm glad to have you here. I'll even make you soup for supper."

"My night gets better and better."

"Don't get too excited. It's from a can. I just have to heat it up."

"If it's hot, I get excited." He winked and then got up to stoke the fire.

And Amelie felt that fire transfer to her chest, where her heartbeats fluttered. She'd opened herself to him, and he hadn't accused her. She could trust him. And she could drop her brave front and allow a bit of the damsel to emerge. Because, truthfully, it was getting harder to keep up the courageous facade. She was being hunted by a killer.

But now her protector was close.

Chapter Twelve

Jason loved a good blizzard. Snow slashing at his cheeks, eyelids and nose. Veins chilled to the bone. Visibility reduced to zero. Good times. But only when he was out having some fun on the snowmobile. When it arrived while he was in the thick of a homicide investigation, he preferred calmer weather.

He secured his snowmobile in the garage out behind the cabin beside the older Arctic Cat model the owners provided for their guests. With a tug of his scarf to tighten it about his neck, he stepped outside. The wind nearly pushed him over. Or it might have been the ice patch in front of the garage door. Steadying himself, he leaped up two feet onto the snow berm that had formed behind the house. There was already a solid foot of powder on the ground, but the wind would lick it up in dunes that could get as high as his hip if the storm lasted through the night.

Boots crunching over the snow, he wandered around behind the log cabin. The snow glittered like diamonds. The smooth surface hadn't had a chance to take on rabbit tracks. Those critters were too smart to be out on a night like this.

And with hope, so would a killer.

On the other hand, if someone did have it in mind to return and finish the botched hit job, Jason wanted it to happen when he was here. Yvette needed protection. And that was something he could do. Even as his better judgment warned him—another beautiful female spy in his life? The last one had changed his life forever, leaving him humiliated and scrambling to prove himself.

This new woman appealed to him both physically and by prodding his innate need to protect. But could he trust her? Her name wasn't even Yvette. And did she know more than she was letting on? How could she *not* know what she had in her head? He wanted to trust her, but it was never that easy. She had been trained in evasive tactics. A man should never let down his guard.

His cell phone rang, and he stepped around to the side of the cabin where the generator was protected from the wind.

"This is Robert Lane. Your dispatcher wanted me to check in with you."

"Hey, Robert, good to have you in town." Robert had helped out last fall when Alex had been sick for a week. The man preferred to move around St. Louis County, filling in, rather than settling in one station. He was good folk. "I'm currently at the Birch Bower cabin east of town," Jason said. "The renter was the escaped perp's target. I want to stay close. Did Marjorie get a trace on the call?"

"Not yet, but I've been looking over your escaped perp's stats," Randy said. "You've got an interesting one, Cash. Looks like a pro hit man. You say you managed to intercept his attack on a woman?"

"Yes. Actually, the victim held her own until I arrived. Surprises me if his stats are so deep," Jason said. "A hit man right here in Frost Falls. Something's not right with this situation. You talk to Ryan Bay?"

"Yes, and he was in contact with Interpol."

"Did they provide information on Jacques Patron?"

"Gave Bay the runaround. Said the assistant director would contact him soon."

"Seriously?" Jason toed the snowy base of the generator. "So he's alive?"

"Interpol wouldn't say anything more than they'd get back to him. Bay was swearing about it."

"Strange. Well. Okay. I'll, uh…" Think on that one when he was inside and warm.

"I'll hold the fort here in town," Robert offered. "Most of the county roads are closed. I don't think anyone will be cruising around tonight, not even on a snowmobile. I might catch a few z's later in the basement. You still got those cozy blankets down there?"

"You betcha. Thanks, Robert. Call me at any hour."

"Will do."

Jason hung up and leaned against the cabin wall. The flurry of snow whipping about darkened the air.

"A hit man," he muttered.

Yvette's boss had sent her out of the country until the heat blew over. Jacques Patron had then called the local police to warn them that his employee was in danger—and, in the process, he'd been silenced.

Or had he? Interpol said Patron would call them soon. Why hadn't they patched him through to Bay when he'd called?

That weird instinctual creep at the back of his neck wouldn't allow Jason to dismiss the boss as dead. Did Interpol really know where he was? Could the call to the station have been staged? To make it seem as though Patron was out of the picture? Because...he was involved and wanted to erase his tracks?

"I need to know what Yvette knows."

But she didn't know what she knew.

"This is crazy."

As THE WIND pummeled the windows in a fierce symphony, Amelie was happy to be spooning up hearty beef-and-vegetable soup with the sexy police chief. Inside, protected from the bitter chill. She hadn't had company since moving here. And despite the reason for his presence, she found herself enjoying simple conversation about snowshoeing on bright winter days.

"The cabin does keep a good stock of outdoor gear," she said when Jason asked if she had problems getting a good fit on the snowshoes. "The mudroom is filled with things like snowshoes, boots and helmets, fishing poles, and a strange long drill that I can't figure out."

"Sounds like an ice auger. There's a lake eight miles south from here. Great ice fishing. I believe the cabin even puts up an ice house for its renters to use."

"There might have been something about that in the information packet, but I'm sure I breezed over that detail. I'm not much for fishing for my supper. I'll take a breaded, prepackaged hunk of cod any day. As long as it's not been soaked in lye."

"Oh, lutefisk. I love that stuff."

Amelie gaped at him.

Jason chuckled and nabbed another roll from the plate and dunked it in his soup. "It's an acquired taste."

Dark stubble shadowed his jaw and emphasized the dimples in his cheeks that poked in and out as he chewed. And those green eyes. They were as freckled as the spots dotting the bridge of his nose. They appealed to her on a visceral level. Due to lacking sexual satisfaction of late—well, she was thinking about a few things she'd like to do with those freckles. Starting with touching each one. With her tongue.

"I challenge you to come out on the ice with me someday," he said. "I bet I can make you a fan of ice fishing."

"I do love a good challenge."

"A woman fashioned from the same mettle as myself." He winked at her.

Could she get swept off her feet by a mere wink? Most definitely.

His phone buzzed, and he tugged it out of a pocket to look at it. "Got a dossier from Marjorie earlier. It's on the perp. I want to finish reading it and…we heard from Interpol."

"Yes?" She leaned forward. If Interpol were actively involved now, she need no longer worry about remaining undercover and could very likely return home.

"Ryan Bay spoke to them. Sounded like they were unaware there were any issues with Jacques Patron. Said he'd contact us in a few days."

Amelie let out an exhale. "He's still alive?"

"Well." Jason pushed his empty bowl forward on the table and clasped both hands before him. "You say you can't make contact with him?"

"No."

"But you've left messages?"

She nodded.

"Sounds like he's avoiding you. If he is alive. And why make such a strange call to the station, and make it sound as though he'd been shot? And yet Interpol also thinks he's alive. Something does not add up, Yvette. Amelie."

"Just stick with Yvette."

He winced.

Because it was easier for her to have him use her alias. Less personal. On the other hand, she could really use a confidant. Someone to trust.

"Maybe it's time I checked in with Interpol," she offered. "That should clear things up. But I know Jacques was keeping this situation dark. If he didn't tell anyone..."

"And why wouldn't he?" Jason leaned forward. "Unless the man is hiding something he doesn't want anyone in Interpol to know about?"

Amelie gaped. A niggle of that idea had occurred to her, but she'd pushed it back, unwilling to believe that Jacques could be dirty. He'd worked so closely with her father. They had been good friends. Jacques Patron would never do a thing to harm her or her family.

"I'll let you think about that one." Jason stood. "Thanks for the meal." He wandered into the living area and plopped down on the couch before the crackling fire.

Amelie caught her chin in hand. She didn't

want to think about it. But he was right. Something didn't add up.

Gathering the dishes, she set them in the sink and rinsed them. A glance to her cell phone saw it was fully charged. To pick up the phone and try Jacques one more time?

He wouldn't answer. She instinctively knew that. Which meant she had already fallen to the side of distrust for her boss.

It felt wrong. She had always been loyal to him and Interpol.

"You going to write up that list?" Jason called to her.

The list was the one thing that might hold a clue to Jacques Patron's actions. She'd write it out and let Jason take a look at it. If that didn't spark any clues, then she'd go over Patron's head and call the director.

Amelie settled into the easy chair before the fire with a notebook and pen, but it was difficult not to notice the man sitting so close. He smelled like the wild outdoors. And he sent out crazy, distracting vibrations that she felt sure hummed in her very bones.

Jason looked up from his phone and asked, "You know the name Herve Charley?"

Startled out of her straying thoughts, she shook her head. "No. You said that is the name of the man who attacked me?"

"Yes. He showed me a license that identified

him as James Smith. The real James Smith—let's see… Marjorie dug up details on him—has been located in the Duluth hospital. He was attacked, nearly strangled. Has been in a coma for days." Jason whistled. "I'll have to call the investigator for that case ASAP. He'll need to know what's going on here. Anyway, our suspect identifies as a known hit man," he read as he scrolled. "No known address in the past five years. But most recent activity has been noted right here in northern Minnesota. I suspect he might be tied to the Minnesota mafia. You ever hear of them?"

"No. Should I have?"

He shrugged. "Interpol knows things."

"Not everything," she replied with a touch of annoyance. He'd grown distant in demeanor since supper. Of course, the man had a lot on his mind. And police work was first and foremost. And yet, she needed to become an active part of this investigation. And the answers could lie in her placing the list onto the paper in her hands.

"Bunch of families in Minnesota all connected," Jason continued as he scanned his phone. "Involved with a gang out of Duluth. We've got a family living nearby at the edge of the Boundary Waters that's into all kinds of criminal endeavors. Poaching is their favorite."

"Is that even a felony here in the States?"

"Misdemeanor. But they're into a lot of stuff, including assault and transporting stolen goods.

Charley has a list of crimes half a mile long, but all minor infractions. Never able to pin the big stuff on him. That's how those guys work. Their lawyers are paid the big bucks."

"So he's a legitimate hit man?" Amelie leaned forward on the chair. "But that's so—"

"Big? Serious? You bet it is. The Minnesota mafia is involved with some European big shots. They handle guns, ammunition, sometimes stolen art. That's common for mafia families."

Unable to focus on what Jason was currently musing over, Amelie raked her fingers through her hair. Because to think about it, why would someone send a hit man after her? For an *invoice.*

She tapped the pen on the blank notebook page. The list she had absently read was so much more. Did she want to know what it really was?

Yes.

Jason scrolled up on his phone. "The Minnesota mafia has strongholds in Marseille, Berlin and Amsterdam. There's your French connection." The man whistled and shook his head. Then he looked at her point-blank. "You sure you know everything that's going on with this forced vacation of yours?"

"Apparently, I know very little. Jacques has all the answers."

"Right. Jacques Patron, assistant director of Interpol, Lyon, France. Marjorie also sent a report on him." He scrolled for a few seconds then swore.

"Wi-Fi just gave out. Surprised it lasted that long. Can you put in a call to Interpol for me?"

"I intend to. But if the Wi-Fi is out…"

"Should still get cell service."

He leaned over and placed a hand on her knee. "I need you to be smart and help me as much as you can." His intense gaze pulled her up from a swirl of emotion, and she focused on those mesmerizing freckled green eyes. "You are strong and brave, Yvette. I saw that when I arrived to find you fending off the attacker. But now you need to stay strong and keep a clear head. Can you do that?"

She nodded. Gripping his wrists, she gently pulled his palms away from her face and yet didn't let go of him. He was warm, and despite the crackling fire, she had begun to shiver.

"I can do that," she said. "I just… Interpol's lack of concern could mean many things. One, they know exactly what happened to Jacques Patron, but they are unwilling to divulge that information. Or they were not aware of a problem until your dispatch contacted him and they are looking into it."

"I'm going with number one. Because they sure as hell would have noticed if their assistant director went missing a few days ago."

She nodded, knowing that was the likeliest of the two. But that still didn't answer another question: Was Jacques dead or alive? If he was dead, wouldn't Interpol call her back in? Had Patron kept her leave a secret to the organization? If so, then that added another suspicious notch to his tally. "I don't understand any of this, Jason. I'll contact Interpol. We need to sort out the facts."

"Thank you." He waggled his phone. "But calls might not be possible right now. I just lost cell service. Until it comes back, if we can figure out what you know, that might help."

"I've got the list right here." She tapped her temple. "I'm sure I can get it out and onto paper."

"Great. I'll stoke the fire and you do what you need to do. Once you get that list written, I'm going to need you to talk to me about your work and anything you can think of that led up to you being sent to a remote cabin in the Minnesota Boundary Waters to hide. Deal?"

She clasped the hand he held out, wanting to not let go, to use it as an anchor as she felt the world slip beneath her. But instead Amelie sucked in a breath and gave him another affirmative nod. "Deal."

Chapter Thirteen

Jason wandered down the hallway into the bathroom and splashed his face with water. He needed a shower, but he'd survive until morning. Heading out here during the storm, he'd known the options would be few regarding sleeping arrangements. He probably wouldn't sleep much. If anyone who wanted to harm Yvette managed to brave the storm, then he dared them to. He'd like to stand against someone with such moxie.

Smirking, he tossed the towel into a hamper and shook his head. Had he been craving some action so desperately that he'd mentally invited a hit man to come at him?

A smart man would wish for a quiet night and a clear morning. With Bay holed up in a motel until the storm passed, Jason needed to get out there and search for the escapee. He didn't like the unknown. He preferred to know every player's position on the board. He was the knight protecting the queen. And somewhere out there the rook could still be lurking. He had to be. His mission to take out Yvette had failed. What sort of hit man walked away from an assignment after failure?

Jason had never walked away from failure.

Until he'd been forced to walk away or risk endangering so many more. It sucked that he'd left the CIA under such circumstances. And now being around Yvette, despite the fact she wasn't an active field agent, stirred his blood for just such fieldwork. He had loved the job—working undercover, researching, tracking and surveilling, and finally apprehending and making an arrest. On more than a few occasions, his objective had been to eliminate a target. His sharpshooting skills had not been exercised lately, but he was confident with his aim. Always.

Despite the mark against him, he'd served the CIA well. As he currently did as Frost Falls' chief of police. Yet losing the perp could be counted as a failure. He should have been the one to take Herve Charley in for booking, and then stand guard.

Maybe he wasn't cut out for this sort of police work?

He shook his head. Stupid thinking. He was just distracted, that was it. And the distraction—another beautiful spy—was his key either to solving this case or, once again, to ruining his career.

"It's finished," Amelie said. "The list." She nodded over a shoulder while wandering into the kitchen to meet Jason at the fridge. She'd left her pen and notebook sitting on the rug beside the easy chair. "You'll have to look at it."

"I will. You got anything to drink in here?"

"Beer and orange juice."

"Beer will work." He opened the fridge. "Now that you've written it out, do you have any idea what the list is for?"

"Like I said, I initially thought it was an invoice. But who kills for an invoice?"

"Not many, I figure." Jason popped open a beer can and leaned against the counter. "You don't know what it means?"

She shrugged. "It can be any number of things. Invoices would normally go directly to Accounts. So I have to believe it was either sent to the wrong email address or, if it was sent to me purposely—"

"It wasn't sent to a wrong address. It freaked the hell out of your boss enough that he sent you out of the country. Someone sent that to you on purpose. Maybe because they knew your connection to Patron and that you would go to him with it."

She rubbed her arms and gave it some consideration. Why would someone want to get to him and do it through her? "Then why not send it directly to Jacques?"

"When involving someone else can twist the screws a little tighter?" he prompted.

The suspicion in his voice troubled her. She hadn't initially thought to suspect Jacques of any wrongdoing. Yet now, all clues pointed to that very real possibility.

"Can I ask what led you to working for Interpol?" Jason asked. "You said something about your parents working for the agency?"

"My dad was with Interpol. That's how he met my mother."

"She worked for them too?"

"No, she was a spy for the Russian FSB. I know, cliché. Not because she chose to, but because she was desperate to protect her family. Her father had been indebted to the Russian government, and he had some black marks against him that the government used to twist the screws. When he grew ill, my mother stepped in and did what she had to do. Which was whatever the FSB told her to do."

"That's tough. But sounds like it ended well? If they met and—she must have gotten away from the Russian government's control?"

"My father helped make that happen. I wish I could tell you my parents lived happily ever after…" Amelie closed her eyes. Memories of that morning flooded back. Her father had been away on assignment. She had been nine.

"What happened to them? If you can tell me. You don't have to tell me," Jason rushed out.

She didn't want to tell him.

She *did* want to tell him. Anyone. Just to release it from her memory. Amelie had thought she was over the grieving—and she was—but it still hurt to think of her mother. And sometimes blurting it out, whether to a stray cat or a cabdriver who didn't speak her language, seemed to alleviate some of the pain.

"My mother was executed," she spilled out.

Instantly, Jason's hand covered hers. His warm fingers curled about hers, and she reactively curled hers around his. "I'm sorry," he said quietly.

"I was nine," she said. "There was a knock at the door. My mother grabbed me and said I should hide. I started to beg for a reason. What was wrong? She said she had done something bad to help good people. I'll never forget that." She met Jason's gentle gaze. "She did something bad to help good people."

He nodded and bowed his head. He understood. It was a spy's lot in life. But a spy's safety was never ensured, even from those he or she worked for.

"I heard a man enter the house," she said quietly. "They exchanged few words." The accent had been French. But her fright and the strain to try to hear the short conversation had kept Amelie from hearing anything more than syllables and sounds instead of actual words.

"My mother cried out. The front door slammed. I knew whoever had come inside the house had left. I waited for my mother to call out again. I waited so long. Then finally I crept out and found her in a pool of blood. It's all a blur after that. I didn't see my father until two days later. He was on a covert mission, and it took that long for Interpol to contact him. I realize now they could have contacted him at any time. They simply wanted him to complete his mission before giving him the terrible news."

Amelie sighed and pulled her hand from Jason's. She wrapped both arms across her chest. No tears. It was what had happened and it couldn't be changed. There had been a formal investigation, but no suspect had ever been found.

"My father died when I was twenty. It was... alcohol poisoning. He drank himself to death. He couldn't handle my mother leaving his life. I almost wished it had been him in her place that day. He was never the same. Doesn't matter now. They are both gone. And I have accepted that."

Jason hugged her, which startled her, but she melted into the warmth of his embrace and managed a smile. She'd never gotten a reassuring hug following either of her parents' deaths. This was a long time coming. She closed her eyes and just let it happen. To feel his heartbeat against hers. To accept that he cared about her. To allow herself to sniff back a tear.

When after a bit he pulled back to look at her, he asked, "You still wanted to work for the government even after all that?"

"I know how things work in the security agencies. Everything is a big secret. Don't tell. Need to know. I signed on for that at a time…let's say I was still reeling from my father's death. But I walked in, knowing what to expect. And that's why I'm here now."

"Gone dark."

"Exactly."

"I'll keep you safe." He squeezed her hand, and his eyes met hers. "Do you trust me?"

"I do. Thank you for listening to my sorry little story."

"It's not sorry. It's tragic. I wish things could have been better for you, Yvette. Amelie." He kissed the crown of her head. He smelled so good. Warm and just so…there.

"I had a great childhood," she offered. "My parents were the best. And you know, they were always honest with me. Telling me they worked for an organization that saved others, sometimes, as my mom put it, forcing them to do something bad. I always had a sort of knowing that something could happen to them. Didn't make it any easier to accept. But it was almost not a surprise, if that makes any sense."

Jason blew out a breath. "My parents are both still alive. Simple, humble dairy farmers. Well, my dad used to be a marine until he had to muster out with a bad back. They are both retired now. And happy. I'm thankful for that."

"I bet having a son working law enforcement makes them both proud and nervous."

"I know my mom was pleased when I, uh… left the CIA."

"You were in the CIA?"

"Not anymore. And that makes my mother a very happy woman, because I could never tell her what I was doing, and the not knowing part is hardest. Now that I'm watching over Frost Falls, she's decided that at least the one son isn't in as much danger. My other two brothers. Well."

"What do they do?"

"Joe works for the DNR. Department of Natural Resources. He's a nature boy, but I wouldn't mind having his daily patrol out on a lake or tromping through a beautiful forest."

"That does sound like a perk. What about the other?"

"Former State Patrol. Uh, Justin got hurt last year. Crazy woman shot him during a routine traffic stop. Left him with some neurological issues. He's doing good though. But that one certainly tried my mother's heart, let me tell you. Mostly, we don't tell Mom about the serious stuff." He cast her a wink. "How you holding up?"

"Honestly? Since I've been staying here at the cabin, I've had a lot of time to think about my life and the choices I've made. Even made up a list of pros and cons regarding returning to my job."

"Which won? Pros or cons?"

"I'm not finished. No matter what I ultimately

choose to do, I don't want to die in this terrible, cold no-man's land."

He smiled at that. "It is terrible in the wintertime, but it's my home. For now, I'm focused on protecting you and solving this case. If there's a killer loose, we'll round him up and bring him in."

Amelie believed him. Even though she knew that if whoever was pulling strings behind whatever was going on wanted her dead, they could make that happen. And she knew Jason knew that, too.

"So you're CIA? Jason, why didn't you tell me that?"

He shrugged. "Haven't known you that long. I'm not much for laying it all out there."

"I can believe that. If I ask nicely, would you tell me about it?"

"Everything you do is nice, Amelie. I like that name. Well, I like them both. But Amelie fits you." He turned and propped his elbows on the counter.

Everything about his physicality fit her just fine. He was so…there. All man, and smelling so good. The sadness over telling him about her parents had slipped away. Hard to stay sad when talking to such a sexy man. Their closeness niggled at her. The idea of tracing his freckles returned, but Amelie pushed it back. He'd revealed he used to work for the CIA. She wanted to know more.

She leaned in beside him. "Tell me what you're willing to divulge."

"That isn't much. You know the drill. I was in the CIA for four years. Circumstances forced me out. That's all I want to say. For now."

He eyed her then, making sure she got his point. She did. Intelligence agencies guarded their secrets. A good agent did the same. Unless she was alone and confused, in a country not her own.

Nodding, she said, "Got it. I didn't tell you my secrets right away. You've a right to yours."

"Thanks for respecting that. You know," Jason said, "all this snow really is a lot of fun. You just haven't done the right things in it yet."

He had dismissed the CIA conversation quickly. She would give him that. For now.

Amelie leaned against the counter, which put her toe to toe with him. "Is that so? Well, according to the instructions left by the owners, I've shoveled, deiced the truck windows and broken icicles from the roof so water doesn't leak in. And I've learned I do like to snowshoe."

"See? That's a lot of fun. You said you take photographs? Or is that just your cover story?"

"Yes and yes. It's my cover, but it's also a hobby I'd like to turn into a career. I'll show you the picture of the moose I told you about." She grabbed her cell phone and tapped into the photographs app. Finding the picture, she turned it toward Jason.

"Wow. That is beautiful. The snow spraying about the moose glitters."

"Magical," she said. "But magic aside, I've dealt with more power outages than a person should have to in their lifetime. And now this blizzard! I guess I'm not seeing the appeal to dressing in layers and learning that sweat freezes on one's eyelashes and upper lip."

Jason laughed. "So does snot. But that's something you learn when you're a kid."

"That's information I will, unfortunately, never lose."

"You remember everything?"

"Most stuff. Not conversations, like this. Mostly data and lists. It's like when you're doing a mindless task and your brain is focused on that one thing? My brain goes into photographic memory mode. I can't turn it off. But if I'm writing a grocery list while I'm running about the house or singing or even chatting with a friend, then no."

"That's cool. What about books and movies? Do you remember them word for word?"

"Sometimes. Again, it depends on my focus and if I'm distracted by friends sitting beside me in the theater. I can absolutely quote every line from the *Italian Job* remake."

"The one with Mark Wahlberg? Wasn't that one the best?" Jason asked. Then he took on a feminine tone, "'My name's Becky, but it's written on my shirt.'"

"'Listen, Becky, I'm gonna need your shirt and your truck.'" She quoted the next line from the popular movie.

The man's laughter was the sexiest thing she'd heard in a long time. Amelie stepped forward, not really thinking, and touched his shirt, dead center over his chest. "Thank you," she said.

"Sure." He clasped his hand over hers. "Just doing my job."

"You're doing more than that. You've given me back the confidence I thought I'd lost since leaving France. You didn't coddle or chastise me after that attack. You said 'good for you.' I need that respect."

"Well earned."

And then she reacted, because it felt right.

The man's mouth was warm, firm and fit against hers as easily as her decision to kiss him had been. She stayed there, inhaling his skin, his breath, his power. One of his hands hooked at her hip and nudged her forward. She pressed her breasts against his chest and then...realized what she was doing.

Amelie pulled away and touched her mouth. "Sorry. I—"

"Please, do not apologize for a kiss," he said. "It'll give me a complex."

"Oh, your kiss was great. Your mouth is so delicious—I mean, kissing you probably wasn't the right thing—"

He stopped her protest with another connection of mouth to mouth. A hot, demanding union that drew up a sigh from the giddy swirl in her core. She settled against him, and when they parted this time, their eyes met. The crackle of the nearby fire mimicked the spark that had ignited in her belly. Everything about her felt melty and relaxed, attuned to his breath, his glance, his subtle nudge of palm against her hip.

Those freckles were like catnip to her purring desires.

Another loud crackle and pop alerted Jason. He looked aside, then pushed her away. "Oh no!" He raced toward the fireplace.

A fire had started on the rug before the hearth. Nothing a glass of water couldn't douse but—her notebook was in flames.

"The sparks must have started it." Amelie grabbed a bowl from the sink and filled it with water.

By the time she made it to Jason's side, he'd stomped out the flames. The rug bore a small black burn in the tight nylon coils. But her notebook was a tattered, ashy mess.

"The list," she said. "It's all gone."

He shot her a direct look. "Forever?"

Chapter Fourteen

The list was a complete loss. Jason had tried to salvage it, but no going. He'd stomped out the fire the spark had started, making sure no hazard remained. Yvette had scrubbed the rug with a towel and tossed the burned notebook. Those old rag rugs made from tightly coiled fabrics always stood up well to stray sparks. They were a northern Minnesota cabin standard.

"The information hasn't been lost forever," Yvette said as she sat on the couch. "But I'll have to start over now."

That was one thing to be thankful for—that she didn't lose the information after downloading it from her brain onto the page.

"I'd appreciate you giving it another go," he said. "It could prove helpful to figure out what the hell is going on."

"Do I have to do it tonight?"

"No." Jason blew out a breath, surprising himself when he felt his muscles stretch wearily across his shoulders. He checked his watch. "It's been a long day. And it's late. It won't matter if you start now or tomorrow."

He sat on the couch beside Yvette. Amelie. He'd better stick with Yvette for the sake of her cover. She'd brought out an extra quilt, and he couldn't avoid the return yawn when he saw hers. Putting up his feet on the coffee table, he settled into the comfortable couch and closed his eyes, pulling the blanket up to his neck.

"I'll sleep here," he said. "I know this cabin has only the one room with two beds."

"You're welcome to one of the beds."

"Thanks, but I like falling asleep before a fire," he said quietly.

"Yes, it is cozy. Do you mind if I sit here awhile longer and take in the ambience?"

"Go ahead."

She sat next to him, and he smiled inwardly. Nice to have the company. And she smelled great. Among so many other things that turned his senses up to ultra-alert. The softness of her skin teased, so close but just out of reach. The accidental nudge of her knee against his. The sweep of her hair across her shoulder.

Outside, the wind had settled some, but Jason expected the drifts to be tall and deep by morning. He didn't mind a good snowing in. Especially when it put him in proximity with a pretty woman. And she had kissed him right before the rug had taken flame. Funny to think, but they had created their own sparks.

He wasn't against making sparks with a beautiful woman. He'd gotten to know her better. She was alone and uncertain. He had known that feeling when first moving to Frost Falls to take on the superfluous job of police chief. But he had made the job his own and was very protective of this town now. Sometimes a guy needed a push in a new direction to restore his energy and positive outlook.

But now that he'd been pushed, he faced the full shove right out of the position he'd grown to love. Damn it, he didn't want to lose this job, as insignificant and quirky as it happened to be.

But he'd be lying if he said he was satisfied living in this small town. Female companionship was hard to come by. He generally dated women from other towns. Not even dates, more just hookups. How to intertwine his job with a happy social life? Marriage was something he looked forward to, but that would never happen if he didn't start playing the field and getting serious.

"About that kiss earlier," he said, eyes closed, content to relax in the warmth.

"I never flirt." She snuggled close against his side. Mm…that contact did not preach relaxation. "I always mean what I say and do."

"Unless you're spying for Interpol."

Her sigh hurt him more than he expected. "I'm

not lying to you, Jason. I trust you. *You.* The guy who confessed to being a spy himself."

"Sorry. You're right. I appreciate that you say it like it is. No playing around."

"There's nothing wrong with a little play."

"Gotta agree with that."

When she twisted and leaned in, Jason tilted his head. The kiss was a surprise, but one he surrendered to like a refreshing free-fall dive into a summer spring. With the fire crackling across the room and casting an amber glow through the evening dark, the mood took on a sultry tone. Yvette's mouth was sweet and seeking. Her breasts hugged his arm. He shifted on the couch to hook his hand at her hip.

This was too good to be real. He didn't want to get his hopes up, but it was difficult not to. Yvette was the sort of woman he would like to date, to have in his life long-term while he learned about her hopes, her dreams, her desires. And could he ever share the same with a woman?

The clutch of her hand at his flannel shirt tugged, insistent and wanting. He glided his hand up over her shoulder and tangled his fingers in her hair. As soft as he'd thought it could be.

The kiss almost went deep and delving, but all of a sudden, Yvette pulled back and smiled at him.

"Good night, Cash." She kissed his cheek, then laid her head on his shoulder.

Mercy. Now he would never fall asleep.

BUT HE DID.

Jason awoke from a snore. The room was dark. The fire glimmered with low red embers. His face felt...cold. As did his feet and legs. Sitting up, he noted Yvette had curled up beside him, her head on the arm of the couch and her stockinged feet against his thigh. There along his leg he felt the most indulgent warmth. But she'd stolen the blanket, and—damn, it was cold in the cabin.

And he could make one guess why.

Getting up carefully, so as not to disturb her, he wandered into the kitchen and opened the fridge. The inner light did not blink on. No electricity. The storm must have taken out the power. Not unexpected. But why hadn't the generator kicked in?

He checked his watch. It was 5:00 a.m. Hell of a time to wake. If he went back to sleep, he would fall into a comfortable snooze but be groggy around six when he normally woke, yet if he stayed up he'd be tired later in the day.

A shiver that traced him from neck to toes decided for him. It was too cold to sleep. But did he really have to bundle up and go out to check the generator?

He glanced toward the couch. A warm body lay there, beckoning his return. Only a few steps away. No need to face the brutal weather.

Jason shook his head. He wasn't one to push the easy button. And if he didn't check the generator now, the cabin would only grow colder, and the risk of the water pipes freezing was a real possibility.

Putting on his coat, boots, gloves and scarf, he worked quietly. Yvette didn't stir on the couch. Yvette, of the luscious mouth. The woman did not tease about flirting. Their make-out session, though too short for him, had stoked a fire within him. He could go there with her. Beyond the kiss and into bared skin and moans. But only as a fling. Because she lived in France and had no intention of staying in Minnesota. And if he started something with her…he didn't want to get his heart broken. It was tough enough being a bachelor in a small town.

Opening the front door and bracing for the cold, he swore silently as his skin tightened. The air hurt his face. Closing the door quietly behind him, he assessed the situation. The snow was not so deep in front of the cabin. Thanks to wind drift, he could still see most of the driveway and up to the gravel road. Here and there, sharp-edged drifts cut across that road. The plow only drove through on Mondays. Which had been yesterday. Though Rusty Nelson, of the gas station, did take his blade through town because The Moose always gave him a free meal in payment. As for the outer, less traveled roads, everybody would have to sit tight. The snowmobile would glide across this fresh powder like a dream.

Walking around the side of the cabin, Jason

navigated the dark dawn with ease. He loved the way the darkness could be bright in the wintertime, illuminated by the white landscape. The world was quiet, blanketed to solace with the glittering snow. The stillness amplified his steps, his rubber-soled boots crunching the snowpack.

He bent and scooped up some snow and tried to form a snowball. It held, but not well. Which meant the snow was not too wet. A good thing if he wished to hop on the cat and ride into town.

Keeping his head down and his eyes peeled, he looked for anything out of the ordinary. Tracks, evidence of anything or anyone who may have attempted to broach the cabin during the night. Cut the electrical power. But the snow cover was pristine.

The back of the cabin was hugged by a snowdrift that reached half a foot up and over the window glass. The two walls that shielded the generator had been worthless. The cover was drifted up high; snow completely covered the generator. Jason swore. Somewhere under all that snow sat the key to getting the electricity back on.

He weighed the options. He could get a shovel out of the garage and dig down and try to figure out what was wrong with the generator. The cabin would not be livable if it had no heat. But he didn't have the time to play handyman. The electrician from Ely, a town about thirty minutes east, would be able to get out here, but he couldn't know if it would be today or in a few days.

The other option was to bring Yvette into town with him. There he could do his job and keep her close until they could find the perp.

Nodding, Jason eyed the garage. No drifts before the double door. Thankful he wouldn't have to shovel his way out, he wandered back around to the front of the house.

THE INVITE TO stay at the police chief's house was unexpected, but welcome. Having woken up shivering, Amelie now kept the blanket tight about her shoulders and wandered down the short hallway into the log-walled bedroom. The idea of stripping away her clothing to shower did not seem particularly wise. Instead, she added another sweater over her shirt and then, with the blanket again draped across her shoulders, pulled on another pair of socks and rolled them to cover the hems of her leggings.

"I really hate Minnesota," she muttered.

Though she was never one to hate anything. It wasn't the state—it was this cold. For certain, France did have its chilly moments in the wintertime. However, she'd become accustomed to working in an office building, insulated from the elements. Maybe the summers here were warm and sunny. In this part of the state, surely the nature must be amazing. She'd only read about the

Boundary Waters and the forest that hugged the upper part of the state, but for an outdoorsman, it must be a dream.

She did want to venture out with her camera again. And if that meant braving the frigid weather, then so be it. Because it was high time she started facing the facts. That pros and cons list? She'd lied to Jason. It had fallen heavily in favor of the cons. And if she was honest with herself, the idea of returning to her current job did not appeal.

Could she make a living as a photographer? It had started as a cover job for her assignments. A good agent tried to choose a cover she was familiar with, so she could easily blend, and Amelie had always loved photography. Thanks to her father's life insurance policy, she had a healthy savings account that would allow her to quit her paycheck job while seeking something that could satisfy her need for fulfilling work. It was something she needed to seriously consider. And soon.

She wandered back out to the living room. Even if she didn't appreciate the current climes, the male species was something to admire. Case in point? Jason stood before the hearth, ensuring all sparks were completely dampened. Bent over in those blue jeans, he provided a great view of his nice, tight—

"You pack?" he called over a shoulder.

"Uh…" Pack? Oh, right. "A few things." She set

down her grocery-run backpack that she'd filled with clothing. "How long do you think it will take to get the electricity working?"

"I'll give Karl a call when we get to town," he said. "Storm dropped a good twenty inches last night. We'll have to take the snowcats into town."

"I'm good with that. For as much as I hate the cold, I actually enjoy dashing through the snow in a horseless open sleigh."

He chuckled. "Good one. You'll learn to like our weather. It's good for the blood."

"It is?"

"Yeah." He slapped his chest, and Yvette could only imagine doing the same, yet gentler, and... under his shirt. "Keeps the blood pumping." His cell phone rang, and he answered as he wandered to the foyer and started pulling on his outerwear. Amelie now realized the Wi-Fi had been available when she'd checked for texts upon rising.

"Yeah?" Jason said to the caller. "You're kidding me? Where?"

Amelie pulled on the snow pants that had been provided by the cabin. They were thermal and designed like overalls, so they provided a layer of added warmth and protection from the elements.

"I'll be there in..." Jason eyed her, then gave her a forced smile before answering the person on the phone. "Give me half an hour." He hung up and then tossed her the knit cap that was sitting on top of his gloves. "Alex found a body in a running vehicle near the edge of town."

"A body?"

"Yeah. Uh…" He winced as he appeared to consider his words. "It's the perp."

"What?"

"Alex ID'd him as the mafia hit man, Herve Charley."

"How did he die?"

"Carbon-monoxide inhalation? Won't know until I can take a look. The medical examiner is already on her way. The main road has been plowed. I'll have to drop you at my house and run. Hell, maybe I should take you to the station. Be safer there."

Amelie pulled on a pout. "I was looking forward to a hot shower. Is your place really a target for crime? And you did say the suspect is dead."

"I thought we'd determined we don't really know what the hell is going on."

Amelie swallowed. He was right. She really needed to get smart about this operation. Because it was a mission she needed to participate in.

"Aw, don't give me the pouty face. Fine. You get a shower. And then you're heading to the station where I, or someone, can keep an eye on you."

Amelie bounced on her toes. It was a small victory, but it lifted her spirits. And she needed that.

Chapter Fifteen

The forest green SUV had been pushed into the ditch. Purposely. It hadn't slid off the icy gravel road while traveling. Though, certainly, the roads were treacherous this bright, sunny morning. Ice glinted like a bejeweled crust under the cruel sunshine. Last night's blizzard conditions had kept every smart person inside and safe in their homes. Save this one. But the vehicle couldn't have been in the ditch for long. The tire tracks leading into the ditch were crisp, only lightly covered with a dusting of snow blown by the wind.

Jason stretched his gaze along the road and spied another set of tracks. Faint, but again, snow had drifted slightly to emboss the tire treads. And they were different than those of the ditched vehicle.

"You see that?" he said to Alex, who stood waiting for Jason outside the patrol car.

"Yep. Another vehicle either forced this one in the ditch, or someone stopped to help but left."

"I'm ruling out help," Jason decided. If it had

been anyone from the town, they would have called dispatch to alert him to the situation. "You run a plate check?"

"Yes. Vehicle belongs to Carol Bradley. She reported it missing from her garage—door open, keys hanging on the key holder inside the garage—forty-five minutes ago."

"Oh, Carol," Jason muttered. "You were just asking for that one. So the perp stole a vehicle that was virtually handed to him in the first place."

Stepping carefully on the icy tarmac, Jason inspected the exterior of the vehicle. Grayish-white dust from the salted roads shaded the green paint. Because of the angle the truck sat at, the passenger's side hugging the ditch was buried up to the bottom of the side windows. The engine had been running when Alex had arrived on the scene, and he'd shut it off. And…the back right wheel of the car had sunk into the ditch, allowing snow to cover the exhaust pipe.

"Not good," he muttered. The exhaust had nowhere to go but inside the vehicle.

"Carbon monoxide?" Alex asked from where he was walking to determine that the only footprints were boot marks from him and Jason.

"Looks like it," Jason called.

"Someone could have run him off the road. Guy got knocked out. The other car backed up and drove off. This guy never woke up," Alex conjectured.

"We'll see."

With a lunge, Jason stepped up onto the running board edging the driver's side of the truck. He peered inside and found exactly as expected. The driver, Herve Charley, was immobile, buckled in, his jaw slack. Alex reported that he'd initially opened the door and shaken the man but had quickly realized he was dead, so then he'd stepped back so as not to contaminate the scene.

Jason stepped down and opened the door, having to push it with some strength to fight against the angle at which the vehicle was tilted. Sliding between the door and the car frame, he leaned in and inspected the guy's face. He didn't notice any bruising on the forehead or temple areas where a sudden slam of the brakes might have sent him flying forward into the windshield. And to know if his chest had hit the steering wheel hard would require the medical examiner.

Charley's eyes were closed. His skin was still pink, but his lips were bluing. Carbon-monoxide poisoning did not tend to blue the skin, and, if Jason recalled a few previous experiences with the like, the lips turned bright red. Certainly, the cold could be a factor in the odd skin color. A heater didn't do a person much good when the wind whipped the icy air through and about the steel vehicle.

He wouldn't touch the body without gloves. The medical examiner would chastise him for that. No visible weapons. No pistol, no knife. He couldn't have purposely parked at such a strange angle, and halfway in the ditch. Maybe he had slid a ways and Jason had read the tracks incorrectly. Because why would someone run him into the ditch? Who knew this man was in Frost Falls? Had he started a fight with someone?

Didn't make sense. He'd escaped from jail. Charley should have been lying low or long gone from the town by now.

He scanned the truck's interior. On the passenger seat sat a plastic grocery bag. When Jason lifted the edge, he spied inside a half-full plastic bottle of a bright blue energy drink and an opened pack of salted beef sticks.

Turning the key in the ignition to get power but not spin the engine, Jason listened to the radio station. It was the Duluth top hits channel that played current songs all the way back to the '60s and the '70s. He checked the gas gauge. Half-full. No other warning lights.

Had Charley been staking out Yvette? He was parked a mile out on the east road, which led to the Birch Bower cabin. Nothing else out this way, save the rental cabin. But what had stopped him from proceeding to the cabin? The road, while slick, was not drifted over. Easily drivable at a slow speed. Had he seen Jason head out this way on the snowmobile earlier in the day? Waiting for him to leave? Possible.

But the additional set of tire tracks bothered

Jason. They had stopped right behind the SUV. No boot tracks, though. Whoever had driven the other car had not gotten out. Alex's guess about another vehicle pushing this one into the ditch, then taking off, could be right on.

Switching off the ignition, Jason stepped out of the truck as Elaine pulled up in the medical examiner's van. Must be her turn to drive the vehicle. The county shared one van between the four offices in the Boundary Waters area.

"The victim did not get out of the vehicle," Alex reported. With a gesture toward the SUV, he added, "He's wearing those cowboy boots. I checked. No tracks outside to match. Just our boots. Although, with the ice and drifting, even if he had gotten out, those tracks would have been dusted away."

"Thanks, Alex." Jason tugged at his skullcap to cover the tops of his ears. He wandered to the rear of the vehicle and inspected the chrome bumper. Sure enough, a sharp dent crimped the end. "Someone pushed him into the ditch. But I feel like he might have been parked here."

"We got a vigilante going after the bad guy?" Alex asked.

"No one knows about our resident bad guy," Jason said.

Except Yvette. But he'd been with her all night. And while Bay and Marjorie knew to keep a tight lid on police business, he could assume the three women he'd questioned about Yvette Pearson's death had already released that information into the gossip grapevine.

He waved as the medical examiner approached. "Elaine! You made it."

Already snapping on black latex gloves, Elaine executed careful steps over the icy road. "I'm a hardy sort, you know that, Cash. Icy roads don't intimidate me." With a nod to Alex, she stomped across the snowpack to peek inside the cab. "Sitting here overnight?"

"Alex found him on morning rounds. He always checks on the Enerson couple down the road."

"That couple must be pushing a hundred, the both of them," Elaine said.

"Einer turned a hundred and one last week," Alex called as he wandered back to the patrol car, most likely to retrieve a thermos of coffee.

Jason wished he'd consumed some coffee before coming here. He'd even suffer the bitter, dark stuff Alex tilted down like an addict. He'd pulled up to his house on the snowmobile, Yvette behind him. Handing Yvette the key to the front door, he'd told her to make herself at home. The last time he'd given a woman free rein in his home, she'd put pink pillows on his couch and had suggested he get a juicer. All he could do was shiver at that memory.

Elaine put up a boot on the SUV's side runner,

and Jason grabbed her elbow to steady her while also holding the car door open with his shoulder.

"Thanks, Cash. You think it was carbon monoxide?"

"I do. But there's damage to the back bumper and additional tire treads. Someone nudged the vehicle into the ditch."

"Interesting," she muttered out from inside the cab.

While waiting for Elaine's initial inspection of the deceased, Jason watched Alex tilt back the thermos. The one thing Jason never missed was his morning coffee. But this morning had been unusual in that he'd woken snuggled beside a beautiful woman. Both of them fully clothed.

Something wrong with that picture.

On the other hand, he never expected anything from a woman unless they had communicated clear signals to those expectations. It had been sweet to find Yvette's warm body curled up against him this morning. Shared body heat on a stormy winter night. Nothing at all wrong with that.

But what did it mean for their future? Why was he even thinking future about the woman? Was it because she was the first woman he'd met in a long time who hit all his *this feels right* buttons? Or was he desperate and lucky to find a beautiful woman, about his age, in the same vicinity as he was?

No, it wasn't that. She was smart, courageous and in need of his protection. And the courageous part appealed to him. A woman who wasn't afraid to defend herself and could take his garbage? Could he get more, please?

A future would be great. Even if that only entailed the two of them getting to know one another better and doing more than sharing a snuggle. An official date would be a great start.

Elaine jumped down and tugged off her gloves then stuffed them in her left pocket. From her right pocket, she pulled out thermal gloves and slid them on. "No telltale cyanosis. Which means it wasn't carbon monoxide. Though it may have lulled the deceased a bit."

"What's cyanosis?"

"Skin turning blue."

"Right. I noticed that, but, well…" Jason peered inside the cab. The body sure looked as if it had suffered from inhalation of a poisonous substance. He adjusted his stance, pressing back the door with his shoulder, but also fighting the whipping wind that suddenly decided to sweep the snow up and into their faces. "What did you see, Elaine?"

"Did you notice the fine crystal on his collar? And the smell of his breath?"

"I didn't get that cozy with the guy."

She smirked. "That's why I get paid the medium bucks. Cyanide poisoning is my initial assessment. I can only confirm with lab tests. But I don't think he took his own life. Which may coincide with the dented bumper and extra vehicle tracks. Someone might have wanted to ensure he was dead."

"I'll call Ryan Bay and have him come out to help us process the scene," Jason said. "Things will go much faster. Then we can all get back to a warm office."

"Bay didn't stay in Frost Falls? Didn't you offer him a cell to camp out in?"

"I'm not exactly sure where he stayed last night. He's been cozying up to Marjorie's husband for dumplings a few nights now. Might have earned himself a bed there." Jason tugged out his cell phone.

"Oh, those dumplings." Elaine nodded her head appreciatively.

Jason stepped aside and let the door close with a good push from the wind. He scanned the ground again. His own boot tracks were barely visible for the icy surface, and he followed Elaine's smaller tracks to the back of the vehicle where she stood. The drifting snow covered them quickly.

The BCA agent's phone carried over to messages, so Jason told him where to meet him, then tucked away the phone in a pocket.

He stepped up beside Elaine, who had turned her back to the wind. She looked out over the snow-packed field, which gleamed with sunshine. "So now we've got a hit man's killer running around town?"

"This case is starting to get very interesting," Elaine said. "Mystery. Thrills. Murder. I gotta say it does add some excitement to the usual natural-causes pickups. These parts, the elderly tend to drop like flies. But you see one death because of age or cancer..." She shrugged. "You've seen them all."

"Not sure I should be glad to oblige your need for excitement, Elaine."

She smirked at him. "You love it, too, Cash. I can see that glint in your eye."

He crooked a brow and looked down at her. "My eyes don't glint."

"Yeah? Tell that to your Frenchwoman."

"My French—what?"

She chuckled softly. "Marjorie told me."

Jason shook his head. "The gossip in this town."

"The whole county, Cash. The whole county. When's Bay going to arrive?"

"His phone went to message."

"Could be a while. I'll get the gurney. You guys help me bag and load up the body."

"Will do." Jason headed toward the back of Elaine's vehicle to get out the equipment they'd need.

If the man in the green SUV had been sent to kill Yvette, then why would someone take him out? Had a cleanup been dispatched to take out the inept hit man? Possible. And probable. Anything goes when the mafia was involved. And, very possibly, Interpol.

Uff da. This was getting deeper than the snow.

Chapter Sixteen

Amelie lingered under the hot water. She hadn't had decent water pressure in the weeks she'd been in the country. Washing her hair under the lackluster stream back at the cabin had been a challenge. Now the water blasted her skin and massaged it and—oh. Just. Ohh...

Another bonus? The house had central heating with electricity that worked. Heaven.

After what she determined was half an hour, she decided a good guest would not use all the hot water, so she reluctantly stepped out onto the plush bath mat and wrapped a thick towel about her wet hair and another around her body. Tucking her feet into the slipper-like socks she'd hastily packed, she then wandered down the hallway to the extra bedroom Jason had said she could use.

The room was...some grandmother's creation. It had made her laugh when she'd first walked in to leave her bag. Crocheted pillowcases and bedspread, and the lace curtains were the same off-white as the bed dressings. The furniture was straight out of the '50s with a plain pressboard headboard, and the dresser looked like one of those old-fashioned televisions that, indeed—upon closer inspection—had a record player on one side and the other side fitted with drawers for clothing. So lost-in-the-past yet teasing Twilight Zone. Jason must have inherited the place from a relative. Or so she could hope his idea of decorating style did not include such strange furnishings.

But she wouldn't look a gift horse in the mouth. It was either this or shivering back at the cabin. She did not care to be alone and too far away from the handsome police chief who could provide her protection when she most needed it.

Amelie hated to admit it to herself, but she did like the presence of a strong, confident man. Sure, she'd trained in self-defense. But with the state of her mind and emotions lately, she'd gladly step back and allow him to stand before her if that's what he could do.

Dropping the towels aside and combing out her hair before the full-length mirror on the back of the door, she relished the warmth that did not necessitate she immediately get dressed.

Her cell phone rang, and she picked it up from the bed. No ID, but she recognized the number.

"Settling in?" Jason asked.

"You don't know how much I missed water pressure."

"Did you save some hot water for me?"

"Are you coming home to shower?" Amelie bit her lower lip. That question could be construed as suggestive. But...depending on how he replied, she'd get a bead on his feelings toward her.

"Was that an invitation?"

Score! She turned before the mirror, studying her naked profile. If he came home right now...

"Sorry, I shouldn't be so forward," Jason said. "I, uh, have a lot to do here at the station with this new twist to the investigation. I can't say much more. This is an active investigation. And you're..."

"No longer in danger?"

"Can you come over to the station and we'll talk?" he asked. "I need to wrap my head around as much info as you can provide."

"Can we meet at The Moose? I'm starving."

"I don't know..."

"Sorry. I didn't mean that to sound like a date."

"It's not that, Yvette. I'm just not sure it's safe for you to be wandering around town, putting yourself out there."

"The guy is dead, Jason. What aren't you telling me?"

He sighed. "He is."

"What if I walk over to the station right now and pick up something for us to eat along the way? It's a straight shot. You can stand outside and watch me walk there."

"I've got a better idea. I'll meet you there, and we'll walk back to the station together."

"Great. I could go for a big serving of meat and potatoes."

"You've settled into the Scandinavian aesthetic."

"I know. And I fear for my waistline because of it. Give me ten minutes to get dressed and I'll meet you there?"

"You're, uh…not dressed?"

"Just stepped out of the shower."

A heavy exhale sounded on the line, and Amelie smiled. She'd given him something to think about. And she certainly hoped that thought lingered with him for a long time.

"See you soon," he said quickly, then hung up.

JASON PUSHED ASIDE the evidence bag he'd gathered from the ditched SUV and tapped the plastic. Inside he'd collected Herve Charley's cell phone, truck keys, twenty dollars and a fidget spinner, of all things. Not a single weapon. No gun. No garrote or knife. This hit man liked to get up close and personal with his marks.

Ryan Bay had called. He'd made contact with the FBI. Charley was on their list. An agent was headed to Duluth to stand in on the autopsy right now. And likely they'd send an agent to Frost Falls.

All this evidence would be sent to Duluth for forensics to put it through their tests, and it would be shared with the FBI. Verification that Charley had contact with Yvette Pearson was important to tie the two cases together. Because if not, there could be another killer on the loose. As well, Jason wanted to see what connections, if any, he could find between Herve Charley and Jacques Patron.

It was a hunch. He had no real evidence to link them. But if Patron was the only one who knew Yvette was staying in Minnesota, in a small town with no more than a grocery store and a diner/gas station/strip joint, then that led to one conclusion: Patron had sent the hit after her.

As Jason scanned what little public information he could access on the Interpol assistant director, he remembered Yvette telling him how she'd proven herself to Jacques by reading lists and then later writing them out. A handy skill to have, especially in the spy business. And if the expense for training her for fieldwork had been put out, only to find she wasn't cut out for such harrowing work, then surely the director would want to utilize her unique skill in some form. And he shouldn't be willing to dispose of that same skill for some little infraction.

Whatever she'd read on that list had been confidential and likely hadn't been something Interpol had expected to receive. Someone must have wanted *her* to see it. Could that someone have known of her memory skills? Or was it that they knew she had a connection to Patron? Were they outside Interpol? Or had it come from inside? That made more sense, considering the difficulty of learning about Yvette's skills and then targeting her email specifically. And was the email sender someone dangerous enough to put a hit out on a fellow employee?

This smacked of duplicity. And that grabbed Jason in the gut and twisted. Hard. He knew what it was like to deal with double-crossing spies. And not only his job but his personal reputation had suffered because of it.

Two years ago, in Verona, Italy, he'd trusted the Italian agent who had been assigned as his liaison while he'd been in the city on a critical operation. Despite Jason's trust of his employer at the time, the Central Intelligence Agency, he had never walked into a situation blind. When he'd learned who was to liaise with him, he'd checked her out. Charleze Portello had been with Interpol as a field operative for six years. She spoke five languages, was skilled in various forms of martial arts and had helped take down a billion-dollar counterfeit-antiques operation in Morocco. Impeccable credentials.

He'd never dreamed she'd turn out to be a Russian honeypot sent to learn what he knew and follow him right to the target.

That had not gone down well with the CIA. Which was why Jason currently wore a cloth badge on his coat and sat in a cold office before a computer that should have been bricked a decade earlier.

Leaning back and blowing out a breath, he shook his head. Feeling sorry for himself? That wasn't a Cash condition. His father had taught him better than that. All three Cash brothers were confident and able, and the vein of cockiness infused by their former marine dad ran hot and heavy in them all. Jason had loved working for the CIA. And he would be a liar to say he didn't miss the adventure, action and intensity of the job. But life had decided he was needed in this town at this moment in time. And…he'd accepted that.

But soon enough, that was going to be ripped from his grasp. Was he not meant to settle and be happy? Why did he keep stepping into jobs that weren't meant to last? Was it something he did? He didn't so much love this town as he did the people in it. And while he understood that Frost Falls was small and a police station was no longer a necessity, he'd hate to see it go. It was a town landmark. And who would be there to direct Ole Svendson to put his clothes back on and get off the main drag?

Things had to start looking up. And they were. With forensics reports due from Duluth, Jason might be able to close one case if Charley's DNA could be matched to Yvette Pcarson's evidence.

Unless a new hit man had arrived in town.

Chapter Seventeen

To say that every diner in The Moose was watching Amelie standing next to Jason as they waited for their to-go meals was putting it accurately. All eyes were on them, accompanied by smirks, nods and raised eyebrows. Of course, whenever Amelie cast a glance toward the curious onlookers, they all resumed what they had been doing. Even if it meant completely missing the edge of the coffee cup and spilling down the front of that snowflake-patterned red thermal sweater.

Out of the corner of her mouth, she asked Jason, "Are we a local event?"

"Apparently, we are." His freckles were even more pronounced thanks to the bright white sunshine that beamed through the diner windows. Amelie admired those same freckles in his liquid green eyes. A sight she could take in forever. "What are you looking at?"

She leaned in close and whispered, "Your freckles."

"Stupid things."

"Why do you say that?"

"Never liked them. My brother Justin once tried to scrub them off me. With a Brillo pad."

"What's a Brillo pad?"

"It's made from stainless steel and is used for scouring food off dishes."

"That's terrible!"

"Par for the course when you grow up with two brothers. I served him his just desserts. More than a few times. Hey, Hank!" He waved to a gentleman leaving the diner, who returned a wink as he opened the front door.

"Marjorie's husband," he said to Amelie. "My dispatcher."

She loved his self-satisfied smile. It popped in the dimple on his cheek. It was all Amelie could do not to lean forward and touch that indent. But the townsfolk had been served more than enough entertainment for one afternoon. And, weirdly, the place had gotten packed since they'd arrived five minutes earlier. Had all those texts and whispered phone calls brought in the entire town— some having to forge unplowed roads—to watch their very single police chief flirt with a woman? Or even more exciting, to possibly overhear some news about the murder investigation?

Amelie chuckled and turned a blatant smile to the peanut gang along the counter, who all quickly snapped their heads around to pay attention to their cooling meals.

"Here you go, Chief Cash." The waitress set a bag on the counter and took Jason's credit card and slashed it through the charge machine. "Will that be all?"

"You betcha. Thank you very much, Charlotte." Jason tucked away his wallet and grabbed the bag. When they walked to the door, he waved to the audience who followed their exit. "Nothing to see here, folks! Just having a little lunch."

Once outside, Amelie shivered against the brisk cold, but she laughed as their footsteps made them dodge a heap of unplowed snow in their path and they bumped shoulders.

"Am I ruining your reputation?" she asked as they crossed the street and headed toward the station.

"If there was anything left to be ruined, I might be worried. But you gotta give them something to whisper about every now and then, eh?"

"If you say so. But speaking of reputations... I shouldn't ask, but I have to. Tell me why you left the CIA."

"Do I have to?"

"I did tell you my sad tale."

He chuckled. "Fine. I didn't leave, I was fired. But my boss wanted me to suffer even more, so he 'placed' me—" he made air quotes "—in a suitable job that required filling."

"This job you have now? It's such a small town. I'm surprised there is even a police station in it."

A passing station wagon honked, and Jason nodded and gave the driver a wave. "Frost Falls used to be four times the population it is now. Wasn't even three years ago it was booming. Workers from the iron range lived here. Then the Red Band iron mine went bust, and everyone packed up and left. It was a lot of migrant workers, but many locals as well. Since there was already a police station, the chief of police stayed on as he watched the town's numbers dwindle. He died of natural causes two years ago. And when they should have closed the station and left the law enforcement to the county, some smart aleck in the CIA decided he'd send one of his agents here as a means of punishment to watch over the peanut gang."

"Did you have to take the job?"

"No. But it was a job, and it's located within an hour's driving distance of both my brothers and my parents, so… Hell." He stopped at the corner of the redbrick station house and looked straight at her. It was his hefty sigh that told her his truths were valuable. And she would handle them with the care they deserved. "At the time, I wasn't in a mental place where I was willing to stand up and fight the system. I was real down on myself and decided to take my punishment as due."

"Punishment for what?"

"I botched a mission."

"Is that all? But…agents do that all the time.

Well, not all the time. But it happens. Backup measures are usually in place—"

"I let a known terrorist walk out of my cross-hairs," Jason said firmly. He closed his eyes and swallowed. "Because she got to him first."

"She?" Amelie noticed the muscle in his jaw tighten. "An Interpol agent?"

"How'd you guess?"

"You were not pleased to hear I worked for Interpol. I had no idea at the time, but that explains your reaction."

"She was using me the whole time. I thought she was a liaison provided by the Italian head-quarters. Turns out Interpol wanted their hands on the target for their own reasons. And it wasn't to take him out. I want to believe it was some kind of trade to the Russians. Far as I know, the target is walking free. It's not right."

"A lot of what goes on in international and national security agencies isn't always deemed right. But who is the judge of what is right and wrong? There are many situations that can be viewed both ways."

"I know that. One man's freedom fight is another man's misdirected protest. The target had taken out women and children, Yvette. Dozens of them. His weapon of choice was pipe bombs placed at coffee shops in the Washington, DC, area. It was a malicious and vulgar crime. I hate myself for letting him walk."

Amelie knew now wasn't the time for argument or reasoning. It was a challenge dealing with the power an agent wielded. Certainly, she had been faced with many such challenges. And ultimately? She'd not been able to pass the cruelest test. To shoot or not to shoot? She'd not realized which side she fell on until it was almost too late. Fortunately, she'd been able to step away and still retain her job at Interpol.

Jason had been punished for something that hadn't been his fault. One of her own had tricked him? Likely a honeypot sent in to cozy up to him, earn his trust, learn what he knew, then report back to headquarters. It happened all the time.

"I won't betray you," she said. "Promise."

He nodded but didn't say anything. He didn't need to. Thanks to his training, and his experience in Italy, he couldn't trust her. Not completely. But she was prepared to earn that trust.

"Thanks, Jason. You didn't have to tell me that. I appreciate that you did. It's freezing out here." She managed a face-crunching smile, then ran ahead and grabbed the station door and held it for Jason.

"Jason." A woman with frosted brown hair cut close to her scalp stood from behind a desk. Must be the dispatcher he'd mentioned. "This must be your French—er, uh, Yvette, wasn't it?"

Amelie tugged off a mitten and offered her hand. "Nice to meet you. You must be Marjorie."

"You betcha. You two dining in Jason's office?"

"You know we are," Jason said with a tone that indicated he wasn't about to take any of the woman's sly teasing. "I'm waiting on a call from the FBI," he called as he entered his office and held the door for Amelie. "Patch it through when it comes, Marjorie."

"Will do, boss."

He closed the door, and Amelie took the food bag to set their meals out on his desk. "Do I get the grand tour?" she asked.

"Uh, sure, but this old station house is the least interesting place in the whole town."

"Oh, I don't know. Marjorie's Christmas decorations certainly do brighten up the outer office."

"They stay up until Valentine's Day, and then we have hearts until St. Patrick's and—it's never boring out in reception. Okay, then! Here's the tour. This is my desk. This is my computer. This is me. That's my deer rack collection." He pointed to the two racks, each more than sixteen points, hanging on the far wall. And next to it hung… "And that is the calendar the print shop in the next town makes of local heroes—they donate profits to the Camp Ripley charity."

"Is that man standing beside a real wolf?" Amelie bent to study closely the calendar hung from a bent two-inch roofing nail. It featured a sexy, bare-chested man with dark hair and a six pack that competed with his incredible dimples.

"Yep, that's my brother Joseph. They call him the Wolf Whisperer. I told you he works for the DNR and has an intimate connection to nature, wolves especially."

"I love wolves. They have such a history. Have you heard of the Beast of Gévaudan in France?"

"Can't say that I have."

"It's an eighteenth-century werewolf legend."

Jason chuckled. "Sorry to disappoint, but there are no werewolves here in Minnesota. You like that kind of stuff?"

"What kind of stuff?"

"Werewolves and vampires and all that weird nonsense?"

She cast him a flutter of lash. "I wouldn't chase a sexy vampire out of my bed."

"Yikes. You women and your…weird fascination for all things…weird. I don't understand why having some fang-toothed monster gnawing on your neck is supposed to be romantic."

"Well, I'm not much for being gnawed myself. Are you on a month?" She flipped up a couple pages of the calendar.

"I was in last year's edition."

"Doesn't surprise me."

This time she took him in from head to just there below his belt. Heh. Was the man blushing?

"I'll have to see about finding a copy," she said. "Especially since beefcake is another of my interests."

"I think my mom has ten. Or a hundred. So that's it. My office," he said. "Pretty exciting, eh?"

"I like it all. Quaint, but underneath it all I'm sure there's a vibrant and busy law enforcement team ready and willing to protect its citizens."

"Always." Jason thrust back his shoulders. "Now let's eat and then get to work."

"Is the food that terrible?"

Jason's voice summoned Amelie from thoughts that were far too deep for what should be a pleasant lunch. Forcing on a smile, she shook her head. "It's too good. I could get used to this home-style cooking. And that's the problem."

"I've never had a problem with a turkey and gravy sandwich."

"I can see why. It's…mmm…so good."

Jason leaned forward and caught his cheek in a palm. "Could a turkey sandwich entice you to stay in Frost Falls longer than you'd planned?"

"My gut answer? Yes." Amelie squeezed her eyes shut. Had she just said that? And the reason it had come out so easily was because there was an excellent incentive for sticking around: freckles and a sexy smile. But. "But I didn't have a planned end date for this stay. And I'm not sure I can survive this place much longer."

"You've been cooped up in that cabin for weeks. Anyone would go loony bin. You should give some consideration to sticking around awhile. Let me show you how to enjoy a Minnesota winter."

She ran her tongue along her upper lip. Not an offer any sane woman would refuse. "Don't you have a girlfriend, Jason?"

He winked at her. "Does it look like it?"

"No. But that makes me wonder why."

He crimped a brow.

"What's wrong with you?" she said on a teasing tone.

"Not a lot of young, single women here in Frost Falls. Or haven't you noticed?"

"Isn't the Saturday-night stripper single?"

He shook his head and chuckled softly. "What about you? Is there a boyfriend back home in France?"

"There isn't."

"Yeah? So what's wrong with you?"

"I work too much and have no social life. But no cats yet."

"That's a good thing."

"So now—" she leaned in closer over her take-out container "—the burning question."

"Shoot."

"Are you interested in me, Jason?"

"Hell, yes."

"I like a man who knows what he wants." She sat back, pleased with that quick and confident answer.

The intercom buzzed, and Marjorie said, "Ryan Bay is on his way."

"Thanks, Marjorie. Bay is with the Bureau of Criminal Apprehension. He'll want to talk to you," he said to Amelie.

"Sure. Standard procedure."

"Nothing to worry about."

"I'm not worried. I've done nothing wrong."

"Nothing except attract a hit man to Frost Falls."

"Is that an accusation? I'm not sure I care for that."

"Sorry. It's not your fault." He set down his sandwich and leaned forward. "Why would someone take out a hit man?"

"Mafia, right?"

"He was a hired gun. Connected to local mafia. And now he's dead," Jason said.

"You said the vehicle was stuck in the ditch. Was it forced off the road?"

"Yes. There was a dent on the bumper and tire tracks indicating that. But the driver wasn't dead when he hit the ditch. Maybe? I initially assumed carbon-monoxide inhalation. Happens in these parts during the winter months. Car slides off an icy road, gets half-buried in the snow. The driver takes the safe route of not venturing out in a blizzard and doesn't know the safety precautions for staying in a vehicle when trapped in the cold. Gotta remember to check the exhaust pipe if you're letting the engine run to stay warm. Doesn't take long for carbon monoxide to enter the brain and lull the person to sleep. For good."

He pulled off the plastic cover from the coffee cup and sipped. "But the medical examiner spotted signs of poison."

"Poison? Why would someone take out the person who was supposed to kill me?"

"I don't know. That's what I'm asking you."

She detected an accusing tone and didn't like it one bit. Sitting up straight, Amelie took another bite of her sandwich.

"You don't trust me?" she asked.

"I really want to." He challenged her with a steady gaze. Damn, those freckles would be her undoing. "But I know very little."

"I know even less. I'm as confused about all this as you are."

"Every thought I have about this case leads me back to Jacques Patron."

"But he's..." She paused. No confirmation of his death had been given. As far as she knew, he could be AWOL. Could he be a double agent?

"Did you have a chance to write out the list while at my place this morning?" he asked.

"No, I'm sorry, the hot shower seduced me."

She caught his appreciative nod with a subtle lift of brow.

"I intend to get to that as soon as we're done here," she said. "Promise. I want to help you. And if there is someone wandering Frost Falls who is so dangerous as to defeat a hit man, then…" She set down the last corner of the sandwich and tucked her shaking hands between her legs. "I'm a little scared."

"Don't be. I will protect you, Yvette. Amelie."

"I know you will." She stood and gathered her container and plastic utensils and put them in the bag they'd come in.

She turned and wandered toward the window overlooking Main Street, trailing her fingers along the scuffed sill. "I suppose a town this size doesn't see hit men all that often."

"You better believe we don't." He tossed his things in the bag and joined her.

His presence softened her fears. Standing so close to him, she felt lighter, safer.

"Thank you for what you've done for me, Jason." Her gaze met his, and her lips parted softly. "I mean, Chief Cash."

Heartbeats thundered as memories of their kisses resurfaced. She moved closer so their legs touched. "You kissed me yesterday at the cabin. A girl might expect another…"

"Nothing wrong with a kiss. And if I recall correctly, you were the one to initiate the kiss on the—"

She kissed him quickly, pleased at his surprised response as his open arms slowly and assuredly wrapped around her back. He felt right pressed against her.

His fiery kiss quickly melted the ice that had taken up under her skin like permafrost since moving to Frost Falls.

She giggled.

Jason pressed a finger to her mouth. "Quiet. These walls are as thin as paper. Marjorie will hear."

"That's all right!" Marjorie called out from the other room. "I'm happy you finally have someone to kiss, Chief Cash!"

Amelie gaped, then muffled another giggle.

Jason raised a brow as if to silently say, "See?"

Amelie's cell phone rang, then immediately buzzed, indicating the caller sent a text message instead of waiting for her to answer. She stared at the screen ID and blinked. Her heartbeat thundered. She opened her mouth but no sound came out.

"What is it?" Jason asked.

"It's a message."

"Yeah?"

She turned the phone toward Jason. "It's from Jacques Patron."

Chapter Eighteen

"I thought he was dead." Jason took Yvette's phone from her and read the message to himself: You there?

"I should text him back." She reached for the phone, but Jason clasped his fingers about it. "Jason?"

"I'm not sure about this. I know what I heard on that message. It was a gunshot."

"That doesn't mean anyone was harmed or even died."

"True. But the guy hasn't contacted you since you arrived—what—two weeks ago? And now he does only *after* the hit man has failed? This doesn't feel right."

"You think that's a text from someone else? Using Jacques's phone?"

"Not sure. I want to do a trace on this text."

"I thought your dispatch came up with nothing on the first trace to your phone?"

"She did, but it's worth another try. Can I take this with me?"

She was beautiful when she was thinking. Bright blue eyes unfocused and head tilted slightly down.

She nodded. "Okay. I don't have any important information on it. Just a few calls to the grocery store and, of course, to Interpol in Lyon. I'll write down my password." She grabbed a napkin, and Jason pulled a pen out from his inside coat pocket so she could write it down.

He took the napkin and wrapped it once about the phone then slipped that and the pen into his pocket. "Just to be safe. If he's alive, that's good, right?"

"But if he is, don't you think I should return his call soon?"

"Let me answer with a different question. If you don't return his call, will the man think you're dead? And more important—will believing you are dead please him?"

She worried at her lower lip with her teeth. Thinking again. Which was exactly what he needed her to do. Everything about this situation seemed to point the compass toward France, and Yvette's boss.

"I'm not stupid," she said. "It could very well be as you suspect. I'll wait until you can track the origin of the text. If it came from Jacques's phone…"

"Interpol wouldn't confirm Patron's death. If they don't know what Patron is up to, they could have begun an investigation of their own. Which means it's possible they don't know where you are. Patron hasn't told anyone. That doesn't sound like standard procedure when an agent goes dark. At the very least, it's noted and the director would know, yes?"

Yvette nodded. "You're right, I don't know Jacques as well as I think I do. And I have a list I need to get out of my head. Once again."

"It could be key to solving this case," Jason said.

AMELIE SETTLED ONTO the chair behind the police chief's desk with a blank sheet of paper before her.

Jason breezed back in from reception, tucking away his cell phone in a coat pocket. "You going to be okay for half an hour by yourself?" he asked, zipping up his coat. "Alex and I are meeting Bay to go over the medical examination on Charley's body."

He wandered over and stood beside the chair. He smelled like fresh, clean air. His overwhelming presence lulled her into a swoony smile.

"I will be with Marjorie standing guard out in reception," she teased. "This shouldn't take too long. What will I do when I've finished?"

"If I'm not back, you can..." He looked around the office, then opened the bottom desk drawer to reveal the contents. "I've got provisions. Snacks and Sudoku. Marjorie will talk your head off it you let her, and she's got a lot of work to do this afternoon. Think she's going to head downstairs and do a little cleaning in the cells, too."

"I won't bother her. Sudoku, eh?"

"For stakeouts."

She lifted a brow in wonder.

"Eh." He shrugged. "I might get to use that book someday. There's always hope."

He leaned over, and when Amelie sensed he was going to kiss her on the top of the head, she quickly tilted her head to catch that morsel against her mouth. He didn't hesitate, finding their connection like a pro. The man pushed his fingers up through the back of her hair, holding her gently. He tasted like all the things she needed right now. Safety, connection, intimacy.

Releasing a tiny moan as his kiss deepened in exploration, Amelie twisted and moved up onto her knees. She spread her hands up the front of his coat, wishing it were anything but the thick black waterproof fabric. Like bare, hot skin. Could a girl get a little taste of that?

Sliding down her hands, she felt the hard shape of his gun hugging his ribs, and then, at the bottom of his coat, she pushed her fingers up underneath it. The Kevlar vest he wore was solid, but thin. His flannel shirt hugged the top of his jeans and…oh yes, there.

He smiled against her mouth, then with a glance toward the closed door, turned and whispered, "You doing some investigation work of your own?"

"I am. And I found what I was looking for." Hot, bare skin. Tight, hard abs. A dangerous tease. "I wish you didn't have to leave."

"You make me wish the same thing." He nuzzled his forehead against hers. "I'd take you along with me, but this is police business and..."

"I get it. I'm not an investigating officer." Amelie took in his scent, his skin, his breath. The moment was so intimate, yet in the background lurked calamity.

With a quick kiss to her mouth, he said, "I'll be back."

"I'll be waiting for you."

"Does that mean what I think it means?" he asked.

"I never flirt."

"You always mean business. I got that about you." He kissed her again, taking the time to make it linger as he swept his tongue against hers and tasted her deeply. Then he swore softly against her mouth, nodded and stood up. "If I don't leave now..."

"I get it. I feel the same. Things are going to happen between us."

"Yes, they are."

"Go," she said. "I'll write out the list. Then we'll...see what happens next."

He strode to the door, pulling a knit cap over his head. "See you soon!"

She waited and waved as he passed before the

front window and strode down Main Street. The man couldn't return to her fast enough. Because he had started a fire inside her, and she wouldn't be able to stop thinking about him until all his clothes were stripped away and that investigation practice turned into real-time experience.

Until then, she did have a more pressing task at hand.

Leaning forward on the not-too-comfy chair, Amelie wrote out the numbers and letters that formed a list she'd viewed weeks earlier in the strange email that she now felt sure had been sent to her with an ulterior purpose. It couldn't have been an accident. Someone had wanted her to take that information to her boss.

And her boss had known exactly what sort of damage that information could do. To him?

More and more, she believed Jacques was involved in something underhanded.

It was slow going this time around because it was difficult to avoid thoughts of Jacques Patron's true intentions. What information was she streaming out onto the paper? It was something worth killing for.

After half an hour, she wrote out the last line. Times, dates, locations and...that mysterious fourth column. Each entry was a jumble of letters and numbers. It had to be code or...maybe a password?

Stretching her arms over her head, she turned

and stood, peering out the window. Jason was still gone, and she hadn't heard a peep from Marjorie after she'd called out that she was going downstairs to straighten the cells.

She wasn't about to go out wandering on her own. But she was antsy now, and the office had chilled noticeably. Pulling on her coat, she dallied with the idea of running down the street to Olson's Oasis for something to munch on. No. Jason had snacks in the drawer. And he'd never forgive her for leaving the station.

Picking up her camera, she wandered out into reception. Amelie trailed a finger along Marjorie's pin-neat desk, taking in the photos of Marjorie and a man with blond hair who must be her husband. A bobblehead of a black cat with green rhinestones for eyes sat next to a desk phone. And a cookbook titled *Hot Dishes* that was flagged with colorful Post-its was splayed open, cover facing up.

She stood back and snapped a few shots of the reception area, being sure to get Jason's office in the background. She'd never been much for interior shots. Nature was most interesting to capture on film. Backing up against the door, she decided a step outside would be worthwhile, because there was a large oak tree that loomed in the back parking lot. And she'd stay close to the station.

Jason's truck was still parked in the back lot, as was a green Honda. Must be Marjorie's. The oak tree's canopy was vast, leafless, and stretched overhead as if an open umbrella.

Tilting back her head, Amelie snapped some shots. Inhaling the crisp winter air, she smiled. Yes, this could become a career that would make her happy.

Chapter Nineteen

"The cyanide killed him," Elaine said over the phone line as Jason scrolled through Herve Charley's cell phone looking for clues. He and Alex stood in the gas station parking lot, where the green SUV had been towed to wait for the Duluth tow to come and take it away. Ryan Bay stood over by his car, on the phone. "I found traces of it in the beef jerky. Clever."

Jason eyed a couple bundled against the day's ten degrees as they passed by, probably on the way to The Moose for some pie. "Whoever followed him must have planted the beef jerky. Probably drove up behind him. Nudged the car into the ditch and waited to see if the driver would react. No reaction. Assumed he was dead, and drove off."

"A fair assessment. The body was clean of any DNA not unique to the deceased."

Jason swore under his breath. They were dealing with professionals. Two of them. One dead. And the other?

"Thanks, Elaine. This may have become an international case. Bay is on the phone with Interpol again, trying to get some real answers about the one suspect that sticks out like a sore thumb."

"Who do you think the perp is this time around?" Elaine conjectured, "A vigilante going after someone who tried to harm another?"

"Why would someone take out a hit man, Elaine?"

"I don't know—"

"Well, I do. It's because the first one has been replaced after a shoddy effort at eliminating the target. Which means Frost Falls has another hit man running loose. The FBI has verified links to the Minnesota mafia right now."

"Which means someone is after your woman."

"She's not my—"

"Where is she?"

"At the station." Jason checked his watch. It had been half an hour since he'd left Yvette. He should check in with her. "I gotta go, Elaine. Thanks for the info."

Dialing Yvette's number, he suddenly jumped when his pocket rang. Alex cast him a wondering look.

"Shoot. Forgot I'd taken her phone as evidence." He patted the pocket and hung up. "I'm heading back to the station. Make sure everyone is all right. Have Bay give me a call as soon as he's off the phone with Interpol."

Jason started walking down the street. For some reason, he quickened his footsteps.

THE SKY WAS white and the sun high. Amelic could even find some good in the cold, because it tingled across her face, making her feel alive. The idea of spending more time in Frost Falls to photograph the scenery, to perhaps even venture into the Boundary Waters Canoe Area Wilderness, was appealing. It would be a great addition to her meager portfolio.

Everything felt normal. Yet a weird feeling of dread prompted her to suddenly twist at the waist and scan the parking lot behind the station. She hadn't heard anything beyond the hum of the heater that puffed out condensation from the rooftop of the station. Narrowing her gaze, she took in the surroundings.

JASON RAN DOWN the street toward the station. His rubber-soled boots took the snow compacted on the tarmac with ease. Four blocks and no one was going to break a sweat in this frigid weather. By the time he reached the parking lot, he cursed when he saw Yvette's figure standing against the hood of his truck.

What was she doing outside?

"Yvette!"

She turned and waved.

Jason spied the flash of red as it glinted across the hood of his truck. "Get down!"

Racing toward the truck, he lunged forward, gripped her by the shoulders and knocked her down to land on the snow-packed tarmac. Their bodies rolled, and he barreled over the top of her. The camera she'd been holding clattered across the snow. Protecting her body with his, Jason looked up and around the front of the vehicle.

"Someone just shot at you," he said. "I was right." He pulled out his gun and switched off the safety. "There's another hit man in town."

Chapter Twenty

"Stay down," Jason demanded to the woman beneath him on the snow.

Yvette nodded. Her eyes were wide, but he detected more common sense than fear in them. She'd been trained for hostile situations.

He scrambled around to the end of the truck bed and crouched low, pulling out his gun. He swept a look around the rear taillight. No movement in the parking lot. Aiming out into the parking lot, he didn't spy the shooter.

Jason's exhale fogged before his face.

The growl of a snowmobile engine firing up alerted him. He sighted a flash of silver that would place the machine in the alleyway behind the antique shop two buildings down.

"I'm going after him!" he called to Yvette. "Get inside the station!" His protective instincts forced him back to the front of the truck where she now crouched. "You got this, yes?"

She nodded. "Go!"

"Tell Marjorie to call Alex here."

His snowmobile was parked ten feet from the back door. Firing it up, he navigated forward out of the parking lot and to the alleyway. He waited until he heard the other snowmobile reach the intersection of Main Street and the corner of the block. The driver was dressed all in black. No cap or earmuffs, and he didn't wear gloves.

"Not a resident," Jason confirmed.

Confident that whoever drove the snowmobile was the one who had shot at Yvette, he gunned the throttle and his sled soared forward just as the other snowmobile took off through the intersection.

Gun tucked in the holster at his hip, he would not fire on the shooter until he could confirm he was indeed the suspect. Worst-case scenario would see him chasing a kid out for a joyride. But his gut told him this was his man.

Picking up speed as he passed through the intersection, Jason saw the suspect turn and spy him. Jason performed a circling motion with his hand, signaling the man to pull over. A press of a button on the handlebar turned on the police flasher lights.

That resulted in the suspect kicking it into overdrive.

Jason had expected as much. He was a hundred yards behind but intended to close the distance before they got too far out of the city. On the other hand, he was an experienced snowmobiler, and even if the suspect had some skill handling a sled, he wasn't dressed for a ten-degree day or a race through the frigid air and newly drifted snowpack.

The road heading north out of town had been plowed by Rusty Nelson early this morning. Jason's machine soared along the hard-packed snow that had formed on the tarmac. Perfect track for racing snowmobiles. In these conditions, he could handle this six-hundred-pound machine like a dream.

He thought momentarily of how close Yvette had come to taking a bullet. Why had she been standing outside? He'd seen her camera on the ground. Taking photos? He should have been more clear about her staying inside.

Was the shooter a replacement for the previous hit man? Dirty business, that. But all was fair in spies and deception. If that was what was going on.

Jason had been capable of such dirty dealings. Once, he'd been sent in to replace an inept field asset, but termination had not been a requirement. And yet the same could have happened to him after he'd missed the kill shot. He'd been taken in so easily by the female agent. Had truly believed she was on his side. Damn it!

He gripped the handlebars and ripped the throttle, cutting the distance between himself and the shooter.

Had Interpol issued an official agent termination order for Yvette? Because she had read sensitive data? It was possible yet highly unlikely. But if so, her boss was either trying to save her neck or cut her throat.

The suspect veered from the main road and took off across the ditch. Snow sprayed in the sky, glittering against the too-bright sun that proved deceptive in that it wasn't able to warm this frozen tundra.

They headed northeast. That direction would not allow an easy escape.

The falls, the town's namesake, sat half a mile ahead. Frozen this time of year. Always fun to take the cat out on the slick riverbed, but if a person didn't know the area, the falls could prove dangerous. He and Alex put up orange warning flags and stretched a bright orange safety fence before the falls, but it seemed every few years some unfortunate soul crashed his snowmobile or took a flight over the falls, which dropped twenty feet to boulders below.

AFTER JASON LEFT, Amelie squatted near the tire for a while. Back flat against the front quarter panel and palms against her forehead. That had been a close call.

She should have never been out here to give the shooter such opportunity. Taking pictures, of all things.

The glint of something silver caught her eye.

She crawled toward the pushed-up snow that demarcated the edge of the parking lot in front of the truck. Something was wedged into the snow.

She started to touch it, then got smart. Pulling her sweater sleeve down over her fingers, she used that as protection to grip the object and pulled it out.

This was what had been fired at her. A dart with a red tip.

"Not cool," she muttered, because the implications were creepier than if it had been a bullet.

Springing up, yet staying bent and low, she crept over to the building, plucking up her camera along the way, and then around to the front door. She quickly went inside and rushed to Jason's office to close the door. Marjorie must still be downstairs tidying up the cells.

She pulled open Jason's desk drawers and in the second one spied some plastic evidence bags. Dropping the dart into the bag, she then sealed it.

Patting her hip for her phone, she cursed the fact she'd given it to Jason. She looked around the desk for a weapon, but there was only a locked gun case with one rifle in it.

There was another hit man?

Of course, they wouldn't let this rest without eliminating the target. Whatever this was. And whoever they were.

As she settled into Jason's chair, fingers gripping the arms tightly, Amelie asked herself plainly if Jacques Patron were friend or foe.

Her father had valued his friendship with Patron. And her mother—well, she didn't remember her talking about the man. Perhaps she'd even avoided him. Amelie recalled a few times when her mother had bowed out of joining her father over drinks with Patron at a local taproom.

Had Patron gotten into dirty dealings? Was he protecting himself?

And was he dead or alive?

Chapter Twenty-One

The falls loomed ahead. In the summer, it was possible to walk from the creek above, using a jagged rocky trail, to the gorge below where the water fell softly and landed on mossy boulders. There were no nearby trees to block the wind or even provide handholds. It was a tricky descent without snow and ice.

In the wintertime? Only an idiot would try to land at the bottom starting from the top. And more than a few did in search of Instagram-worthy shots of the spectacular frozen falls. The smart ones wore crampons and used rock-climbing gear. The stupid ones? Jason had rescued a handful of injured climbers over the past two years. Couple of broken arms and a head injury from falling ice chunks. The fine was two thousand dollars if he caught the culprits.

But right now he was more concerned about the one idiot who had no idea what waited for him. Snow blanketed the land as far as the eye could see, and the whiteness played tricks with the eye, disguising ridges, valleys and even edges where the land stopped. The suspect would drive his snowmobile right over the falls' edge if Jason didn't intervene. The last thing he needed was another dead hit man on his hands.

Gunning the engine, he pushed the cat to full speed and gained on the suspect. Veering right, he cursed that he only wore a ski cap and no helmet as the snow spraying up from that move spat at his bare cheeks like pins. He paralleled the suspect, who pulled out his gun and fired at him.

The bullet went wide. Jason wasn't worried about being a target—not at this speed. He jerked his machine to the left, forcing the other to veer left. Gauging he had less than fifty feet before the snowy land gave way to a twenty-foot fall, he stood and tilted his body to pull a tight curl. The nose of his sled butted the other snowmobile's nose, and the impact caused the driver to fall off in a soft landing.

Jason gunned the cat and managed to slip ahead of the other snowmobile and clear it before that machine, unmanned, soared over the falls. His own machine skidded up a cloud of snow behind him as he wrestled it to a stop but two feet from the falls' edge.

Muttering an oath worthy of this annoyance, Jason shut off the snowcat and pulled out his gun. He headed toward the man, who struggled in the knee-deep snow. Difficult to find purchase in the fresh-fallen powder. Jason stomped through the crusted surface, wishing for snowshoes.

"Hands up!" he called.

The suspect pulled up an ungloved hand. Sunlight glinted on the gun he held. Jason pressed the trigger but didn't squeeze hard enough to release. He held steady.

The shooter's hands were too cold. Trembles gave way to jerky shudders. The gun dropped out of his frozen fingers. It sank deep into the snow. The suspect's knees bent, his body falling forward. His face landed in the snow as he struggled against the freezing elements and the inability to keep his body warm enough to stand upright.

AMELIE ANSWERED THE landline on the desk the moment Marjorie opened the office door and popped her head in.

"Hello?" Amelie said. She waved at Marjorie to indicate she stay put.

"I've apprehended the suspect," Jason said. "Just wanted to make sure you were safe."

"I am. Marjorie just got in from downstairs. I'll tell her to contact Alex now."

Marjorie signaled with an *okay* shape of her fingers and left for her desk. Amelie heard her say Alex's name.

"I'll be there in half an hour," Jason said.

She nodded. "You should know he wasn't shooting bullets."

"What?"

"It was a tranq dart." Amelie eyed the evidence bag; a few drops of water had melted from the snow on the outside. "He wasn't trying to kill me. It would be a strange weapon to use if death was his objective."

"Interesting. Someone wanted you incapacitated—he had to have been following you. Waiting for…"

"For me to make a mistake and walk outside, giving him a clear target. I'm so sorry, Jason."

"We'll talk when I get in."

"I finished the list," she added quickly.

"Excellent. See you soon."

THE SUSPECT WAS not speaking English. And it wasn't a Texan drawl this time. Jason knew very few French words, but he did recognize the language. Interesting. For about five seconds.

Patience did not come easily today. He was frustrated and yet invigorated at the same time. This was a mystery. Something he'd been wanting since taking the desk here in Frost Falls. If he was going to prove his worth, this was the case to do it. The powers that be wouldn't want to close the station after he'd solved such a big case. This would put Frost Falls on the map. He'd prove he was an asset to the town as well as the county.

Beside him stood Ryan Bay.

"You recording this?" Jason asked.

Bay nodded and pointed his cell phone toward the prisoner. "Go ahead."

Jason turned to the prisoner, who sat on the bed in the cell, head bowed. "You used a tranquilizer dart," he said. The prisoner lifted his head. The man understood him. He had to if he had made his way around the United States to Minnesota from wherever the hell he'd come from. "You didn't want the woman dead?"

The suspect tilted his head subtly, then bowed it again.

"Who do you work for? The Minnesota mafia?"

The prisoner smirked but neither shook his head nor nodded in confirmation.

Then Jason tried a hunch. "Interpol?"

The slightest tensing of the man's jaw told Jason so much. He'd hit on something. He exchanged a raised eyebrow with the BCA agent, who nodded.

Was this hit man really on the same team as Yvette? Jason had to search the Interpol database. With the fingerprints he'd taken upon booking him, he could do that search. But if he was from Interpol, and the previous hit man had not been—what was going on?

Alex wandered down the stairs, and Jason asked, "Did Marjorie run the fingerprints?"

"She's still trying to upload the scan. Sorry, Cash. Won't be much longer."

The station still used the old card-and-ink method of fingerprinting. Which meant they had to upload a scanned image of the fingerprints to run them through the database. What he wouldn't give for the fancy digital scanners all the well-budgeted stations used nowadays.

"I'll check with Interpol," Bay said. "It may cut our time and we won't have to deal with this insolent."

"Good plan," Jason said.

"I get my phone call," the man said from behind the cell bars.

Jason turned at the perfect use of English. The bastard.

"That you do." He took the receiver off the landline attached to the cinder-block wall and handed it through the bars, letting the cord dangle from a horizontal bar. "Alex will assist you with dialing. Good luck getting through though."

He hesitated before walking up the stairs behind Bay. The last time he'd left Alex alone with the prisoner, the man had escaped. Only to be found dead hours later. Jason considered it for a moment. This time the suspect could have his food stuffed through the bars, if it came to that.

He also knew that phone hadn't received any reception since he'd been working here. Maybe a broken wire. Maybe even a frayed cable on the outside phone lines. Too bad it wasn't in the city budget for repairs.

He took the stairs two at a time, following Bay, and stepped out into the frigid air with a brute shout as the brisk chill instantly permeated his flannel shirt. He'd left his coat in the office.

"I'll be right in," Bay said, walking toward his car. "I need to make a few calls."

"You can use my office phone," Jason called, but the man was already rushing toward his vehicle.

Running around to the back door, Jason entered the building, stomping his boots free of snow on the mat.

Marjorie greeted him with a smile.

"You get the fingerprints scanned?"

"Running them right now. The Wi-Fi has been wonky since the storm. But I crossed my fingers and promised my firstborn if it would hold out. The connection is running slower than the old dial-up, but we should have results soon."

Jason swung around Marjorie's desk and eyed the spinning colored ball on the computer screen that indicated it was doing its work. Slowly.

"Miss LaSalle is in your office. I fixed her up with coffee and last year's local calendar. I keep a few copies in my lower drawer. For emergencies."

She ended with a "toodle-loo!" leaving Jason shaking his head. How had Marjorie known Yvette was interested in the calendar?

He knocked his fist against the thin wall as he opened the door to his office. They really needed to insulate these inner walls.

Chapter Twenty-Two

Well, hell. Not like he wasn't proud of the July centerfold that featured him washing the station patrol car shirtless. Heh.

Yvette was seated behind his desk, sipping coffee and grinning widely. Wow. Her eyes actually glinted. Just like Elaine had said his eyes had a glint. Huh. Guess it was possible. And never before had he seen such a bright yet devious smile.

"Hey, I gotta give back to the community somehow, right?" Jason hooked a thigh up on the corner of the desk and leaned over to spy the source of her amusement.

"Marjorie said this was the office copy." She tapped the July spread. "But she already texted me the link to the online version. You definitely go above and beyond with community service."

"I do like to serve the greater good."

"Greater good, indeed." She winked and then covered an even wider smile behind another sip of coffee. "You interrogate the guy who shot at me?"

"He's not overly talkative. Cross your fingers

the Wi-Fi stays connected so we get a fingerprint match soon."

Yvette crossed her fingers, then pointed to the plastic evidence bag at the corner of the desk. "It's the dart that I plucked out of a snowbank. No fingerprint contamination. Promise."

Jason took the item and studied it. "I've seen these in syringe form," he commented. "Used when security professionals are holding down an aggravated target. Firing one out of a gun at a human seems so…"

"Sporting? Like a hunter after his prey?"

"I was going to go with creepy."

He turned the bag to study the dart tip. The only way the shooter could have guaranteed a good placement was to get close to Yvette. Ten to twenty feet maximum. He'd seen the target acquisition red light on Yvette, and yet, he hadn't seen anyone in the area so close. He'd had to have been at least half a block away. Likely, he'd intended to tranq Yvette, toss her over a shoulder— and then what? Take her to crime scene two to finish the job?

"I'll send this to Duluth for forensics to test it. See what this dart contains."

"Jason, I'm so sorry," she rushed out. An exhale preceded a watery look up at him. "I was bored. I'd finished the list. I figured if I stayed right by the station, it would be fine to snap a few shots. I've been so foolish since arriving here.

You can see why I would have never made a good field agent."

"Don't give yourself such a hard time. Nobody's hurt. That's what matters."

He noticed Yvette's subtle shiver. Her discomfort gave him the shivers, too.

"They didn't want me dead. At least, not right away," she said. Her voice trembled. "They want what's in my brain first."

He set the dart on the desk and stood, hooking his thumbs at his belt loops as he scanned out the window behind her. He didn't want her to see his concern, but they both knew how desperate this situation had become.

"The perp is behind bars," he offered.

Yvette sighed. "That's what you said the last time."

That statement cut at his pride. He'd screwed up with Herve Charley. No matter that it hadn't been him watching the prisoner at the time of his escape. Jason took responsibility around here. He had to.

Marjorie beeped the intercom.

"Cash, we got a hit on the fingerprints. And the CIA is on the line for you and Bay."

Really? What the hell was the CIA doing nosing in on the scene? Bay had contacted the FBI. They should have matters pertaining to Charley in hand.

"Thanks." He glanced to the desk phone. He'd

prefer to take the call in private and not with an Interpol agent in the room. "Be right there."

Yvette stood, but he shook his head, gesturing she sit back down. "You stay in here."

The last thing he needed right now was the CIA sticking their noses in his business. They'd controlled him up until they'd dumped him here in Frost Falls. What next?

"Fine." She sat. "But you know how thin these walls are."

He winced as he opened the door and stepped out into reception. Wasn't much he was going to keep private, and especially not with a conference call.

"The CIA?" He looked to Bay, who was nursing a cup of coffee in a paper cup advertising The Moose logo. "Thought you were connecting us with Interpol?"

"I was, but I got a ping from the CIA looking to conference with us. And…here they are." He nodded to Marjorie, who pushed a button on her phone.

"Jason Cash," the man on the line said. "Marcus Fronde, counterintelligence director for the CIA."

Jason knew the man. Not personally, but more than a few times his name had appeared on a dossier for an overseas job. Counterintelligence? They got involved when a foreign entity was in the mix. They must have gotten wind of Bay's call to Interpol. But from the FBI?

There were too many fingers in the soup for Jason's comfort. And the last agency he wanted to deal with was the CIA.

"You've been busy up there in your frozen little town," Fronde said.

"Yes, sir. That's what they sent me here to do. Keep the peace and enforce the law." He glanced to Bay. Surely he'd been briefed regarding Jason's history. He didn't react, merely crossed his arms high over his chest.

"Not working so well, eh?" Fronde said. "You've got a homicide and a dead shooter with known connections to mafia activity in your area."

Jason swallowed and turned his back to Marjorie, who respectfully penciled something on the calendar splayed open on the desk before her. "Keeping an eye on me?" he asked.

"Always. You've got Agent Bay there?"

"Yes, sir," Bay replied. "We're coordinating with Interpol. Or attempting to. The target in this case is one of their agents."

"You realize when an investigation goes international, the CIA wants in?"

Yes, he did. And no, he did not want a CIA agent charging in and taking over his investigation. He didn't mind sharing with the BCA. Bay was nothing but a handy reference should he need his assistance.

But to step aside and allow a CIA agent to do the job he was supposed to do?

On the other hand, they could probably twist the information he needed out of Interpol merely by cachet alone.

"I've got things under control. And with my experience," Jason said, "I know what to do. Though if you can hook me up with a liaison to Interpol, I'd be appreciative."

"Forget the liaison. I'll be sending out an agent. Should arrive this evening. Tomorrow morning at the latest. They'll relieve you of the case."

Jason opened his mouth to protest, but the call clicked off.

He thrust a fist before him in frustration. The urge to swear, and loudly, was only tamped down by pressing his lips together and compressing his jaw.

"I get your anger," Bay said. "I've read your bio."

Great. Just freakin' great.

"I can handle this," Jason said.

"Another set of eyes and ears isn't going to obstruct the investigation," Bay said calmly. "As you said, they will have more leverage with Interpol. Can't understand why they're giving us the cold shoulder, especially when one of their agents is involved."

"Yeah? Maybe two of their agents are in the thick of this."

"What are you thinking, Cash?"

"Her boss, Jacques Patron. He could be pulling strings on his end, covering things up."

"So he's moved to the top of your suspects list? We don't have confirmation that he's dead or alive."

"Right. And that feels twenty kinds of wrong to me. Admit it, that's suspicious."

"It is. So why not welcome the CIA to assist? Come on, Cash, it's all water under the bridge now. Doesn't matter who works the case so long as we get a good outcome."

Jason nodded. "Just hate to see Frost Falls lose this station. You know they're going to shut us down come March, forward all calls to the county?"

"What?"

Jason tightened his jaw at Marjorie's outburst. Shoot. He'd meant to tell her that at a better time.

"Sorry, Marjorie. I've known about it a few weeks. Was intending to tell you. I thought this case might give us some leeway. Maybe even impress all the right people."

"Uff da." The dispatcher sat back in her chair, shaking her head.

"It's not so much the station you want to save," Bay said, "as your reputation. Admit it, Cash. You were a damn good CIA agent. Your sniping skills were highly commended."

"Can we have this conversation some other time?" Jason said with a glance toward Marjorie, who now looked at him like a deer in headlights. "The case is all we need to discuss."

"Sure. But don't get your hopes up about the station staying open." Bay tossed his empty coffee cup in the garbage can beside the desk. "I'm going back down to see if the prisoner may have changed his mind about talking.

"I'll be close." Jason stepped away and into his office, closing the door behind him. Anything to get away from Marjorie's sad stare. But the escape wasn't exactly what he'd hoped for, because Yvette looked up from her place behind his desk.

"What did the CIA have to say?" she asked quietly.

"Uh, just keeping an eye on me."

"They're stepping in, aren't they?"

She'd heard it all. Damn it.

Jason could but nod. He shouldn't take this so hard, but—damn it, this had been his one chance to prove himself!

"Then we'd better hurry," she said. "And figure this out before that happens." She pulled a piece of paper out of her pocket and handed it to him. "The list."

Chapter Twenty-Three

Jason unfolded the notebook page, which still dangled ragged bits from where Yvette had torn it from the spiral binder. The writing was neat but tiny. She'd said she thought it was an invoice. Dates and locations didn't necessarily imply invoice but could rather denote meetings or pickups or even exchange of goods. Something had occurred at the listed location on the corresponding date. Something associated with a dollar amount. The amounts were even, ranging from two thousand to eighteen thousand euros. Some amounts were listed with a dollar sign, which might indicate a difference in who was giving and who was receiving.

"Could be gunrunning," he mused out loud. The Duluth harbor on Lake Superior was one of the largest US outlets for importers of illegal firearms.

"You think?" Yvette exhaled an exasperated sigh. "I hate firearms dealers. They are the nastiest of the nasty."

"Indeed, they are. But it's a guess. Someone was receiving money for…something. At these dates and locations. And some amounts are listed with a dollar sign so I have to figure it wasn't just euros involved. Interesting."

"Then why would *I* have received that email?"

Jason shrugged. "Someone letting the cat out of the bag? Trying to call attention to it without being the one to do so. Could be anything. Corporate shills. Assassins. A list of eliminated targets and payouts."

"You really think it came from within?"

He wasn't one hundred percent sure about that. Or anything, at this point. But his Spidey senses were tingling.

"Your boss," Jason said. "Remind me how he acted when you'd told him you had this info stored in your head."

She leaned her elbows onto the edge of the desk. "Jacques has always been a calm, cool man. Hard to get a read on him. His eyes are gray."

"That have significance? Eye color?"

"Soulless," she said. "And his hair is graying, so he was always sort of…not there. Easy to blend in. Which made him a great agent, I'm sure. But as a fellow worker, I could never get a read on him."

"And yet, I initially sensed you had a good rapport with him? That you liked him? You call him by his first name. That indicates something more than a mere business relationship."

"I did. I do. Like I told you, I remember him from when I was a teenager. I've grown up trusting him. So, yes, our relationship is personal, but on a friendly level." Yvette wrinkled up her face. "But after receiving that message, I'm not so sure what that relationship has become. Is he dead or alive? What's going on, Jason?"

Jason took a moment to put himself in the head of a French Interpol director who knew a woman who carried a list in her head—a list he apparently had read quickly, then burned it. Those were not the actions of a man who had nothing to hide.

Had Patron removed Yvette from Lyon to then make her death look like an accident? Why send her all the way to Frost Falls? What was the mafia connection? Was there a connection? Could Herve Charley have been a random hire? No, he'd read about the French connection in the stats.

"No one knows where you are? No family? A girlfriend?"

She shook her head.

He snapped the paper with a forefinger. Had to be sensitive information. Was Jacques Patron protecting someone? Himself?

"Tell me more about Jacques Patron," he said to Yvette.

A knock on the door preceded "Cash?"

It was Ryan Bay.

"Come in."

Jason slid a thigh onto the desk corner and crossed his arms over his chest.

"Talked to Interpol again and sent them the prisoner's fingerprints. They are cooperating with this information. Still couldn't get any info on Patron. Said they're looking into it." Bay handed him a single printed paper. "You won't believe who we've got below."

Jason's eyes dropped to the prisoner's name: Rutger Lund. Thirty-seven years old. A field operative. For Interpol.

He glanced to Yvette. They'd sent one of her own to take her out? Yikes. How was he going to tell her that? Did he need to tell her that? Yes, he did.

"What's up?" she asked.

"Got the prisoner's name," Bay said to her. "Rutger Lund. You know him?"

She shook her head. "Should I?"

"He's an Interpol agent," Jason said.

Yvette's jaw dropped open. And Bay pulled up a chair to sit down.

"You going to do this, or am I?" Bay asked Jason.

Jason pulled his desk chair back and gestured for Yvette to sit down. "I'll do it."

"You guys suspect me now, don't you?" Yvette sat, and when neither of them answered her, she beamed her big blue gaze up at Jason. "You do."

"Didn't say that," he said.

"Well, I'll say it," Bay tossed out. "We've got an Interpol agent hiding out in Frost Falls under an assumed name…" He handed Jason another sheet of paper from the file folder. "Her real name is Amelie Desauliniers. Has worked at Interpol for two years. Six months in the field and another eighteen—"

"For their tech department. I know," Jason said. "She's told me as much."

Bay stood and leaned his palms onto the desk. This was the first time Jason had seen the fire in him show in his curled fingers and tense jaw.

Jason took an instinctual step toward Yvette. He stood beside her but a step away from touching her. "She was sent here because she had sensitive information in her head that her boss feared could get her killed," Jason said.

"What sort of information?"

Yvette turned the list Jason had set on his desk toward the agent, and he took it and read it. Bay shrugged his shoulders. "What does this mean?"

"Not sure," Jason offered.

"Well, ask her!"

"I don't know what it means," Yvette replied. "It was a strange email that turned up in my inbox. It didn't have an origin, and it self-destructed after a few minutes. But it was enough to put my boss on the alert and want to send me away for a while."

Bay winced. "I'm not following."

"She's got a photographic memory," Jason explained. "She remembers things she reads, like books and lists, but doesn't necessarily know what it is she has seen."

"And you believe her?"

"I'm the one who's been the target," Yvette said firmly. "I'm not on a case, or running a ploy or—I haven't been a field agent for a long time. I'm just trying to stay alive while we figure this out."

Agent Bay scanned down the list. He tapped his fingers on it. "Three columns of data. Looks like a date column, possibly location and…"

"Time," Jason offered.

"But this fourth column is a mix of numbers and letters. A password? For what?" He shot a steely gaze at Yvette.

But she had no answer. If her boss had wanted this out of everyone's eyesight, including his own…

Over her shoulder, Jason asked, "How do you code operations?"

"That's probably need to know."

He gave her an exasperated look. "I'm not asking for state secrets. I'm trying to keep you alive."

"Right. Uh, usually a three-or four-letter sequence. First few letters of the operation code name. If something were called Blacktail, for instance, the code would be B, L, A, C."

"Gotta be a lot of operations that begin with *black*, don't you think?"

"That's true. Maybe I don't know for sure. You think there are operation code names on that list?"

"I don't know. Let me see that list, Bay."

The agent handed it over, and Jason took a few moments to read it.

"This last column for each entry is eight to twelve characters long. It's gotta be passwords. What makes you so sure your boss, who sent you off to a foreign country and then basically left you here without contact, isn't working for someone else?"

"If he was protecting himself, then why not take me out right away?" she asked. "Fire me or have me eliminated that night I went home. Instead he sends me to Minnesota? For what reason?"

"To get you far away until he figured out what to do with you," Bay offered. "And it would it be cleaner to take you out on foreign soil."

"How so? Taking out a target on home territory would be neater, more contained and something a person could control."

"True, but the evidence would no longer be in Interpol's backyard."

"And if my guess about the mafia connection to France is correct," Jason said, "then perhaps he wanted her in his hire's range. Maybe Jacques is a double agent. Or he's protecting a double who has been taking payouts."

"But agencies employ double agents all the time," Yvette said.

"Don't I know it." Jason shook his head and growled at the same time.

"Oh right," Yvette said. "Her."

Bay and Jason exchanged a look.

Jason scrubbed his brow with the heel of his hand. "That's not what we're discussing. Maybe Jacques wanted this information hidden," he tossed out. "Forever."

"Are you implying he had no intention of ever bringing me back in?"

"I don't know. He is the one man who knew what was on this list. And is he still alive?" He looked to Bay.

"I asked and was told that was need-to-know information," Bay said.

"Don't you think that's a little strange?" Jason asked.

Bay shrugged. "Yes, but they have their secrets just like we have ours. They work much more closely with the CIA. Do you think the prisoner in your jail cell knows what the list is for?" Bay said. "He has to."

"Why does he have to? He's only been sent to take out the target."

"He didn't want me dead," Yvette said. "He wanted me incapacitated."

"Right." Jason had forgotten that detail. "So he could then extract what you know. Maybe he does know. And if he's Interpol...something doesn't add up here. Someone knows something. And I need to find out who and what that is. We need to talk to him again, Bay."

"I agree."

"Come on." Jason headed out of the office but called over his shoulder, "Yvette, or Amelie, look over that final column again. See if it makes any sense to you now."

Chapter Twenty-Four

Jason paced before the cell bars. It was cold down here, but the prisoner had not taken the blanket to wrap about himself. A sturdy man, he was about Jason's height and build and had slick black hair and dark eyes. He sat on the bed, back to the cinder-block wall, knees bent. He faced the bars. Marjorie reported he'd eaten every bit of his food. (And Jason would, too; those meals came directly from The Moose.) He was also fastidious about his personal grooming and had requested a book, any book, to read. One of Marjorie's romance novels sat splayed open on the bed beside him. Jason wouldn't even smirk at that. He'd sneaked a peek at a few pages when Marjorie wasn't looking. Those books were interesting.

And written in English.

The BCA agent stepped up beside Jason and gave him a look. Yes, he was ready.

"Interpol, eh?" Jason said to the prisoner.

The man maintained his gaze but said, "I wasn't able to place a call."

And now he spoke English perfectly well. "I know. Repairman has been called for the faulty wiring." Yes, like a year and a half ago. "By law, I'm supposed to report your whereabouts to Interpol."

"That is not correct."

"How do you know? Are you familiar with Interpol procedure?"

The man looked aside, bowing his head.

"Did Jacques Patron send you here to pick up Amelie Desauliniers?"

The man crossed his arms over his chest and tilted his head back against the wall. No comment.

"You weren't sent to kill her," Jason said. "So I have to figure that means you either came to take Desauliniers home—though, why you'd do it in such a covert manner does puzzle me. And if you're not returning her to Lyon, then the only other option is to extract information."

"Phone. Call."

"Like I said, a repairman has been called. Another storm is headed toward us, though. Makes travel difficult. You'd better hunker down for the wait."

"You have a cell phone in your pocket. Desk phones elsewhere," the prisoner insisted.

"I do, but you are not in a position to access them, are you?"

The man crossed his arms tightly and looked aside.

Jason toed the base of a cell bar. "This is what

we've learned from a database search. You are Rutger Lund. An Interpol agent. Home base, Marseille. Seven years in the field. Expertise, black ops. Apparently, covert sniping and operating a snowmobile were not in your training."

"You have no idea what you are sticking your nose into."

Jason propped his forearm against a couple of the cell bars and peered between two of them. "Why don't you enlighten me?"

He didn't mind getting flipped the bird. He hadn't expected the man would engage in a sharing session with him. But he had gotten a roundabout confirmation that he was Interpol. And that only troubled him further.

"I'll let you sit on ice awhile longer." He glanced to the thermostat on the wall, right next to the phone. "These concrete walls are thick, but they don't insulate against the weather well. Talk to you in the morning."

The man swore in French as Jason and Agent Bay headed up the stairs.

UP IN JASON'S OFFICE, Amelie studied the list. With the CIA headed this way, they had their work cut out for them. She knew the CIA would take over the case, and she also knew that Jason would take that as an affront. He hadn't come right out and told her, but he needed to solve this case. A small-town cop planted in the middle of nowhere who had once traveled the world on covert missions? Hell yes, he probably needed this like a person needed oxygen.

And if she could help him, then she would.

She scoured over the paper. Cash payouts? To whom and what for? Interpol was huge and employed thousands across the globe. If this was a confidential list, it could only have been meant for Patron's eyes. The fact she had received it? Someone wanted to out Patron.

Because if it implicated anyone other than her boss, why wouldn't he have acted on that information immediately and—maybe he had.

No. Then there would have been no reason to send her out of the country.

"I'm missing something."

The final column, Amelie had postulated, could be passwords. But for what? Each was associated with a different date, location and dollar amount. Was it a locker that held the payout, accessible only with the correct password? But the dates were all past. Why include the password if the pickup had already occurred?

She closed her eyes and recalled the day she'd opened the suspicious email. Unless she wrote things down, she wouldn't recall it all exactly, but she could remember the layout of the document on her computer. Two single eight-and-a-half by eleven-inch pages. Four columns. The final column…had those characters been underlined?

She opened her eyes. "Like clickable links?"

The email had disappeared after ten minutes. It hadn't gone to the trash file. Not recoverable. Yet nothing was ever completely lost from a computer's hard drive. Security agencies employed talented individuals who could access even the most buried information on a hard drive. It wasn't in her skill set, but the tech manager was certainly qualified.

The first hit man had to have been ordered by someone who didn't want the information falling into other hands.

But as for the suspect sitting in the jail cell below? He'd wanted her alive. And had very likely taken out the first hit man.

Yet her death was for the ultimate reason of… what? If they'd kept her alive, it had to be for a reason. To extract the information she knew? But it seemed as if Jacques might already know that info, so he couldn't be related to the second shooter.

Amelie leaned back in the uncomfortable office chair. She felt at odds and alone, standing in the middle of a flooding room. She had no allies. Even Jason couldn't be considered one. He was only doing his duty. This investigation had begun with the body of a dead woman. An innocent woman caught in a fouled assassination attempt.

She bit her lip. That poor family.

"How's it coming?"

She stood abruptly with the list in hand. "I didn't hear you walk in."

Jason lifted a brow and cast her a discerning look. Even though the look was meant to be questioning, she still swooned at the sight of that freckled gaze. "You figure out the final column?"

"I think these are passwords," she said. "I recall now, on the original document, the fourth column was underlined."

He lifted a brow.

"Like clickable links," she suggested.

"Good going. How do we access the original document?"

"We don't. Not unless we turn this investigation over to Interpol."

"Not a good idea. I have reason to believe someone is involved in a cover-up," he said. "And I'm beginning to think it was cash payouts."

"Payouts to whom?"

Jason shrugged.

Amelie wrapped her arms over her chest and bowed her head. The sensation of tears niggled at her, but she would not cry in front of him. That was not professional. And she had to look at her exile here as a continuation of her job. For her own sake, she had to stay strong and figure this out.

"What is it?" Jason leaned over her and stroked her hair.

His kind touch tugged at her tears, but she

sniffled and shook her head. "I'm sorry. It's all so much. I feel abandoned. Out of place. Feeling sorry for myself, I suppose."

"You have every right. You are alone in a strange country. And a damn cold and inhospitable country at that."

"Why couldn't he have sent me to Florida?" she said with a lighter tone.

"Your boss ever mention friends in Minnesota? Allies? Employees?"

"You think he chose this state for a purpose?"

"The Minnesota mafia does have a connection to France."

Amelie met his gaze. Damn, he was so handsome. Why had she met Jason Cash in such a situation? Any other time, she would have reached to touch those cute freckles on his nose.

He gave her shoulders a reassuring squeeze. "What are you thinking about right now?" he asked.

She set free the smile that was always so close when in his presence. "Your freckles."

He wrinkled his nose. "You spend a lot of time thinking about my freckles."

"They're sexy."

Amelie leaned in and kissed him. She twisted on the chair, and he knelt between her legs. Cupping her head with his hands, he deepened the kiss in an urgent and insistent way. He tasted like coffee. His heat fired within her like no hearth fire ever could.

She gripped his shirt and tugged him closer so she could wrap her legs about his thighs. He bowed his head and kissed down her neck and throat. She almost moaned with pleasure. But she was aware that Marjorie could be in the next room. A few minutes of this pleasure was all she asked.

When his hand brushed her breast, her nipples tightened. And she dared the quietest moan. Jason answered with his own restrained sound of want.

He broke the kiss and pressed his forehead to hers, closing his eyes. He breathed a few times, heavy and wanting, then stepped back and pulled her up to embrace.

"I want you," she said quietly.

He nodded against her head.

"I want this to happen."

"It will," he said in a quiet, low tone that stirred at her humming insides. So sexy to have to be quiet when all they wanted to do was rip each other's clothing off. "Not here."

"'Course not," she said on a breath. "You have an investigation going on."

He gave her another quick kiss. "I do, and it's only just gotten started. Oh, you mean that other investigation? The one regarding the hit man and the French spy?" He smiled. "I prefer the first, but duty does call. Let's solve this case. Save the girl. And then…"

"And then?"

"And then we'll see what happens next."

Chapter Twenty-Five

Snow whisked across the tarmac, plastering the main road thick white. Jason stomped the flakes from his boots before entering the station. He'd walked Yvette across the street to Olson's Oasis after Colette had waved her down. Said she'd ordered a helmet for her and it was in. The two women had started chatting, so Jason had pleaded off and told Yvette no more than ten minutes. He'd be watching the store out the station window.

The station smelled like roasted turkey, gravy and lots of buttery mashed potatoes. Marjorie did not have a meal on her desk. She handed him a cup of coffee as he entered.

"You already eat? You should go home, Marjorie. Storm's not taking its time today."

"I intend to. Just grabbing a few necessaries in case you need me to make some calls while the station is closed. I've already talked to county dispatch. They are on call. I fed the prisoner again."

"I guess you did. A Thanksgiving dinner?"

"*Uff da*, it's freezing down there and we are not Guantánamo. I gave him back the pillow you removed, too."

"Marjorie."

She lifted an eyebrow, and Jason conceded with a nod. "Fine. He's going to have to sit through the storm down there. I'll turn the heat up a few degrees."

"Already done." Marjorie pulled on her bright red parka. "I left some snacks, too. Cronuts and popcorn. He'll be fine. Isn't the CIA headed our way?"

"You betcha. Just heard from them. On their way from the Minneapolis airport."

"Through the storm?"

Jason shrugged.

"I know you don't want them stealing your case," Marjorie said. "Maybe they'll allow you to work with them?"

"Doubt it. Me and the CIA—it's bad blood, Marjorie. Agent Bay shouldn't have said what he said earlier. But I'm not going to pull a hissy fit. If they want to take over, it's their case. But until they get here—and I'm predicting the storm will hang them up somewhere around Hinckley…"

"Good eats in that town," Marjorie said.

"They'll have to hunker down at Tobie's. Best cinnamon rolls this side of the Twin Cities."

"So speaking of all the things Agent Bay has let slip." Marjorie walked up to him and wrapped a scarf about her neck. "You going to tell me more about the station closing?"

"I don't know much, Marjorie. City budget cuts. They plan to close us in March. I thought I could do something, maybe this case would bring attention to us and they'd reconsider, but..." Jason sighed. "I'm sorry."

"It's not your fault, Cash. This station has been on its last legs since the iron mine closed. Maybe it's time I retired, eh?"

"Uff da," he said.

"Exactly. Bay is down with the prisoner. Not sure what he's up to, but that's where he is. Where's your woman?"

"She's not my woman, Marjorie."

"You want her to be your woman."

"Would you quit calling her my woman? She's... I like her. Okay?"

"There's nothing wrong with kissing a woman you want to protect. And now that the prisoner is behind bars, what will she do with herself? Oh, there's a handsome policeman willing to keep her warm on a stormy night."

"Marjorie!"

She chuckled and headed toward the door. "It's not very often I get to tease you, Cash. Let me have this one." She waved and left the station.

And Jason smiled to himself. He'd let her have that one. Because he had gotten the pretty one.

"FIVE MINUTES," THE waitress told Amelie, who sat at the counter nursing a cup of coffee. "I need to let the pie thaw a few minutes before I cut it."

Amelie had ordered a couple of slices of pie for herself and Jason. A surprise. The Moose was close enough to the station, and she'd scanned the area. Hadn't felt a sense of unease. She'd be safe by herself for the time it took to finish this cup.

"Pass the sugar."

Amelie startled when the woman next to her at the counter asked for the condiment. She noticed her sitting at the counter when she'd walked in. Her coffee cup was half-full. She was beautiful. Dark black hair was cut choppy just below her ears, and lots of smoky eye shadow drew attention to her gray eyes.

A perfectly groomed eyebrow lifted in question as she silently stared at Amelie.

"Oh, yes, sorry." Amelie slid the sugar shaker toward her. "My mind was elsewhere."

"Probably on the crazy weather, eh?"

She had a definite French accent, Amelie thought. Not unusual in this town, for she'd learned that many passing through came from Canada. French Canadians traveled down to Minnesota to shop because the exchange rate was so good. Add to that, the Boundary Waters Canoe Area Wilderness was a gorgeous vacation site.

"I'm getting accustomed to the weather," Amelie provided. "What about you? New in town?"

"Just passing through. The hubby and I are headed for Canada. Relatives. You know."

"That's the accent I recognize."

"Yours sounds French, as well. But not Canadian. What part of France you from?"

Amelie felt a sudden and distinct twinge in her gut. That instinct alarm that she had been trained never to ignore. Of course, the woman was simply making conversation. While talking to another woman her age, not from the area, sounded like heaven, it was weird that someone would be passing through during a storm. On the other hand, these Minnesotans were a hardy breed, and a few flakes never kept them in one place for long.

"Refill?" The waitress filled the woman's coffee cup and then looked to Amelie.

She shook her head. "I'll be back. I'm headed to the, uh…" She pointed toward the corner that turned into a long hallway leading to the restrooms.

"I'll go check on the pie right now." The waitress walked off.

After a sip of her coffee, the woman with the dark hair beamed a smile at her. Amelie felt that grin on her back all the way down the end of the counter. Even after she rounded the turn, it burned up her neck.

Why was she getting this feeling? Simply because the woman wasn't from around here? Amelie wasn't, either. Still, most travelers would plan ahead in such weather.

With the bag containing the helmet in one hand, she pushed open the bathroom door and paced before the stalls. The strong lavender air freshener gave her a sudden headache.

The same kind of headache she got whenever she thought about Jacques Patron.

Turning to push open the door, Amelie caught it roughly against her palm. She stepped back to allow the new person to enter. With an "excuse me" on her tongue, Amelie stopped speaking at sight of who it was.

"Hey, sweetie." The beautiful woman with the smoky eye shadow grinned at her. Except this time, Amelie didn't need instinct to know that grin was malevolent.

JASON PICKED UP the list that lay on the desk before him and wandered to the window to peer out. Main Street was clear. Back to the list. Jacques Patron was protecting someone who had been taking bribes or kickbacks. That was his conclusion. It made sense. A date, a location for pickup and a dollar amount.

Of course, the list could not be something Patron had made himself. The only reason a person would make such a list—and put it in the hands of an Interpol employee—had to be for blackmail or push. But why involve Yvette?

Jason honestly did not believe she had a clue what she was involved in. She wasn't lying to him. She couldn't be. So that meant someone knew she had a relationship to Patron and that upon seeing the list, she'd go to her boss. And he'd known what it meant as soon as she'd shown him.

He felt sorry for Yvette. All her life she'd known the man only as a kind friend of the family. And now he had betrayed her.

Did it matter who Patron was protecting? He could be protecting himself, for all Jason knew. What did matter was that an innocent woman had gotten trapped in the middle, carrying information she hadn't asked to know in the first place. And now someone wanted her dead.

He tapped the last column on the list. Clickable links? To what? Videos? Of? The person accepting payoffs?

"Makes sense."

The only people who had any clue what was on the list were Yvette and Jacques Patron.

Jason had heard a gunshot at the end of the message Patron had left him. Yet...he hadn't heard a human grunt of pain following. Most people vocalized when shot, even if it was just a moan. Which meant...

"He's still alive." Had to be.

Interpol was generally open with information

when asked through the correct channels. And yet, if an investigation into one of their own was underway, they would likely keep that close to the vest. As Jason had done. But if the CIA had already stuck their noses into this, there could be information that Jason wasn't allowed to know.

Time to go with his gut.

"Patron is protecting himself," Jason decided. And he knew it was true.

He checked his watch and frowned. It had been twenty minutes since he'd left Yvette at Olson's Oasis. He glanced down Main Street again. Where was she?

Jason grabbed his coat and soared out of the office. Only to come face-to-face with a smirking man in a black suit, wearing no outerwear. His shoulders crouched forward against the wind.

The CIA had arrived.

Chapter Twenty-Six

Amelie came to with a snap of her head upward. Ouch. She sat upright and blinked. Where was she? She had been in the ladies' restroom at The Moose and—the woman with the gray eyes had walked in and smiled at her so wickedly.

A shiver crept along her arms. She wore no coat, just a sweater, jeans and boots. Taking in her surroundings, she didn't hear anything, but—what was that? Wind whipped wildly against the windows that filtered in hazy light. The storm sounded angry. The concrete floor was littered with dust and debris. She sat on a wood chair with flat side arms, and one of her wrists was bound to that arm. Her other wrist was free, but her arm sat heavily on the chair. She didn't feel tied up, not at the ankles or around her waist or chest. And to test, she slid forward on the chair.

"Not so fast, sweetie. I need you to relax."

Her instincts had been right. The woman had

kidnapped her and taken her...somewhere. How much time had passed? How had she gotten her out of The Moose? She must have had help.

Scanning before her, Amelie took in a vast, empty building. Looked like an old garage, the kind used for fixing cars. There were two big doors through which cars could drive in and out, and a small walled-off office toward the front. One window with yellowed glass was frosted over. But no tools or furniture, save the chair she sat on and a wood table beside her. Actually, the table was a plank of plywood sitting atop two wood sawhorses. A makeshift operation.

"Where am I?"

"I honestly don't know," the woman replied. "Some abandoned garage. This town is overrun with empty houses and buildings."

Her accent no longer carried the Canadian cadence.

"Who do you work for?" Amelie had the clarity to ask. She still hadn't seen the woman. She stood behind the chair.

"None of your business, sweetie."

"I am not your sweetie. Do you work for Jacques Patron?"

The woman laughed and walked around to the side by the table. She set a pistol on the plank and lifted what Amelie now noticed was a syringe. A spill of black hair fell across her left eye and cheek as she studied the clear plastic tube on the device.

"You haven't figured it out yet?" the woman asked.

"If I had, I wouldn't be sitting here right now."

"You do have the list in your head. That's what I've been told."

"I…" She wasn't going to provide information when it wasn't clear what the woman knew. "What's your name?"

"Hey, if you don't want to be friendly, sweetie, then names are off the table. Let's quit with the girlfriend chat. It's cold in here, and I'm sure you'll want to get some warmer clothes on when we're done."

"Does that mean you're not going to kill me?"

"If I kill you, I'll never have access to what you know."

"You don't have access to it now. What's going to change that?"

"This." The woman held the syringe closer to Amelie. "Sodium pentothal. It'll make you tell the truth."

A drug used to obtain information from unwilling subjects. "It might relax me and make me tell you who my secret lover is, but how will it extract information you don't even know about?"

"You tell me."

"About my lover?"

"I'd slap you, but I'm not as cruel as you think.

It was a necessary evil bringing you here on the sly. And as for secrets? The whole town knows you're sleeping with the police chief. *Dieu*, he's a handsome one. Now let's get serious. You're going to tell me what was on that list. Line by line."

A snap of a fingernail against the plastic syringe brought Amelie's attention up and to the left. She met the woman's gray irises. She didn't know what the drug would do to her. It was supposed to relax a person's inhibitions and even make them suggestible. But would that also unlock the things she stored in her brain? Things she was normally only able to release by writing them down? A physical action that worked as a sort of dictation machine from brain to hand to page.

"I don't think it'll work," Amelie said as firmly as she could.

By all means, she'd like to stay alive. And if retaining the list in her brain could do that for her, then she would talk her way around it until they were both shivering from the cold.

Where was Jason? Could she hope he'd sense something was wrong and find her? The town was small, but as the woman had said, there were many abandoned buildings and houses. Too many for Jason to go through one by one, and in the storm.

How long had she been out? He must have missed her by now.

"I have to actually write out the information,"

she tried. "Which means I'll need paper, a pen and probably a whole pot of black coffee."

"That's not the way this is going down." The woman's grip on her arm felt like an ice princess personified.

Amelie struggled. She was basically free, save for her left arm being tied down to the chair arm.

"Sit still or this needle will end up in your eye!"

A male voice alerted them both. "Leslie Cassel."

Both women stopped struggling. Amelie squinted to eye the man who stood near an open door, which let in bright light and snow flurries. He was not Jason. Yet she recognized him immediately.

"She's going to bring you down, Patron," the woman—Leslie—said. "We've been on to you for weeks." She stabbed the needle into Amelie's arm.

"Can't risk Interpol learning about my indiscretions," Jacques said.

A gunshot sounded. Leslie screamed. And Amelie grabbed for the syringe, still in her arm.

Chapter Twenty-Seven

Blood spattered Amelie's cheek. Leslie had been hit, and she'd dropped to the floor behind her. Had it been a kill shot? She did not groan, nor did Amelie hear her moving. But she wasn't in position to turn and assess with Jacques Patron standing thirty feet away with a pistol aimed at her.

She glanced at the syringe she'd dropped on the floor. The plunger had not been depressed. *Merci Dieu.*

"What the hell is going on?" she asked, more out of anger than fear, or even a desperation to make conversation and delay the man's likely goal of shooting her. Out the corner of her eye, she spied Leslie's pistol that lay two feet away on the wood plank.

"Doesn't matter, does it?" Jacques had a calm manner to his speech when he spoke French. An affectation that had once reassured her. Now it made the hairs on the back of her neck stand upright. "I hired an idiot to do a job I should have taken care of in Lyon."

Jason had been right. Jacques had been protecting himself all along. Amelie's stomach performed a squeeze, and her heart dropped. Why Jacques was hesitating was beyond her. He was a skilled operative who had never paused to pull the trigger when called for.

"You don't want to kill me," she said calmly. "If you did, you would have done so, as you've said, right away in Lyon. Is it because you don't have the list?"

"Oh, I know what's on that list. I thought I could make it go away by sending you away. After all, you are Vincent's daughter. We were friends. But then I got smart."

"I still don't know what's going on, Jacques. And if you think about it, that means you are the only one with all the facts. You can trust me. Let me walk away from this."

"You may not know." He redirected his aim toward the floor near her feet. "But they do." He fired again.

Behind her on the floor, Leslie yelped and cursed.

In the commotion, Amelie grabbed the gun from the table. She stood. Her left wrist was still bound to the chair, but she could take aim and defend herself.

She heard Leslie's body shift on the concrete floor, as if she were dragging herself.

Jacques laughed and splayed his hands up near

his shoulders, the gun barrel pointing toward the ceiling. "Go ahead, Desauliniers! Take your best shot!"

Never had mockery cut her so deeply. Because he knew…

"Tell me why you did this," she insisted. Her aim targeted the man's heart. "What do I know?"

"He's been taking hush money from the mafia…" Leslie said from the floor. "They're running guns through the Superior Lakes. Patron is their French connection. You're our only proof… Amelie…" Leslie gasped. Coughed. "What's…in your…head. A list with links to security videos showing Jacques accepting payoffs."

How did she know so much? And she knew her real name. And Jacques. Apparently, she was investigating him. And had tracked his connection to Yvette here to Minnesota…

"She's with…" Amelie quickly did the math. Jason had mentioned the man they had behind bars was an Interpol agent. He must have had a partner. "Interpol. Because you know her," she said to Jacques. "You called her by name. And she didn't kill me because they need me to—" Jacques took aim at the floor again. "No!"

Another bullet fired. With a hard bite on her lower lip, Amelie realized she hadn't fired the gun she still held in defense. Not even to protect Leslie.

No sounds from behind her this time. Had he killed her?

Amelie stretched out her arm, willing herself to pull the trigger. Yet a tear threatened at the corner of her eye. He'd killed Leslie. The man had lied to her. Had used her. And had sent a hit man after her. The same killer who had murdered an innocent woman. And now Jacques was here to finish the botched job.

Her fingers clutched the weapon surely. Why couldn't she pull the trigger?

Images of her mother flashed before her. She hadn't told Jason the entire truth. Scared and wanting to know if her mother was all right, Amelie had sneaked out and into the living room, crawling behind the sofa. The man who had entered hadn't noticed her. And she'd seen her mother. Kneeling on the floor, head up and pleading with the stranger who Amelie could never see or reconstruct in her memories.

Amelie's life had never been the same because someone had pulled the trigger and ended her mother's life.

She never wanted another daughter or son to know the loss of a parent. No matter their crimes.

Jacques's chuckle was unnerving. The man was unhinged. If he had been taking bribes and had sent a hit man after her, then he deserved to die. And yet, Amelie wanted him to pay for his crimes. Most importantly, for the innocent woman who had died by mistake, and for killing the woman lying on the floor behind her.

"I'm waiting," Jacques cajoled with a tormenting tease to his tone. "You can't do it. You father would be very disappointed in you, Amelie. You couldn't cut it as a field agent because you couldn't pull the trigger. What makes you think you can do it now?"

She didn't want him to be right. But—what was wrong with her? All she had to do was pull the trigger. She had been an ace aim in training. She didn't have to kill him. She could aim for his shoulder so he'd drop his weapon, and then send another bullet into his thigh to incapacitate him.

Yes, she could do that. Maybe?

Jacques shook his head and tutted as if she was a child. "Just like your mother. On her knees and unable to defend herself when the stakes were at their highest."

"My mother was assassinated," Amelie yelled in English. She didn't want to play nice with the man anymore. "Wait. How could you know she was on her knees?"

Jacques's smirk curdled Amelie's blood.

"No," she said with a gasp. "You?"

He shrugged and nodded, before saying in English, "She was a liability to your father's work."

"You bastard!" The gun suddenly felt three times heavier. It slipped in her grasp.

And Jacques chuckled. "You can't pull the trigger!"

"She doesn't need to," called out another male voice. "Because I can."

Chapter Twenty-Eight

The target turned toward Jason.

Jason had heard him talking to Yvette. It was Jacques Patron. Very much alive. And that man intended to kill his own agent. He wasn't sure if the woman on the floor was dead. Or what had gone down in the conversation that had all been in French, save the last few lines. But it all stopped now.

He'd panicked when Yvette had not returned to the station. He'd raced to Olson's Oasis, and Colette had said she'd seen her stop in at The Moose. There, the waitress had told him about the unfamiliar woman with the great hairstyle and how she'd followed Yvette into the bathroom. It had been easy enough to follow the trail of a woman's boot prints—deeper in the fresh-fallen snow because she'd been carrying a load—and to the tracks that had led toward the south end of Frost Falls, where a string of abandoned shops and businesses had sat empty for years.

As Patron raised his arm to fire off a shot, Jason

squeezed the trigger. No waiting. No pausing to allow the villain his "this is why I did it" speech. Just take him out, efficiently and quickly. No foreign double agents to redirect his focus. But Patron was damn well going to live to answer for the crimes he had committed against his agency and Yvette.

Jacques yelped and clutched his thigh with his gun hand. Not a direct hit on the femoral artery. Jason didn't want him to bleed out. But a painful strike that should lodge in bone.

Another shot landed in Patron's shoulder. The bullet entering muscle and bone brought him to his knees. Still, he held the gun. And managed to fire. The shot went high, pinging a steel ceiling rafter.

This time, Jason aimed, breathed in—and on his out breath he squeezed the trigger. The bullet pinged Patron's gun, sending it flying from his grasp to land spinning on the floor six feet away.

With the hostile disarmed, Jason ran forward and kicked the gun he'd wielded toward the wall. Out of his peripheral vision, he saw Yvette struggle with the leather strap binding her wrist.

He rushed to help her. "Are you okay?"

She nodded. "Check Leslie. The woman on the floor. You didn't kill him."

"Didn't need to. Don't want to." Jason tugged out his cell phone and hit a speed-dial number. "Alex."

"Yes, Cash?"

"You locate Bay?"

"You betcha. We're waiting for orders. The CIA agent is wondering where you've gotten to."

Jason had told the agent he had to run out to his truck for something and to make himself at home in his office. He could have used him for backup, but—hell, he'd needed to move, and fast.

"I found the perp, Alex. Come to the old Reynolds Repair garage south of town."

"Will do, Cash."

Seeing the strap about Yvette's wrist was actually a thin leather belt, Jason helped her get out of the clasp. She gripped his forearms as if to steady herself.

"You sit," he said. "Take the gun." He nodded toward the pistol on the plank. "Keep an eye on Patron. Can you do that?"

She nodded. She was flustered, but he had confidence she could hold a gun on her boss. Another bullet wasn't required to subdue him. Yvette could maintain her innate need to not harm another human being. No matter what the man had done to her.

Jason bent to inspect the woman on the floor. A bullet had nicked the side of her neck, and she was bleeding profusely. Her eyelids fluttered.

"She's alive." He tugged out his phone again and dialed. "Alex, get an ambulance on the road as well. Call Ely. Bob Hagar drives the ambulance. He can navigate this storm like Rudolph through a whiteout."

"On it, Cash."

The woman had taken a bullet to her shin as well as the thigh. With some field triage, Jason could keep her stable. Shedding his coat, he unbuttoned his flannel shirt and pulled it off. He needed to put pressure on her neck so she didn't bleed out.

The woman's eyes fluttered. Briefly focusing on his bare skin, she said, "Nice."

With a smirk and a shiver now that his bared chest had taken on the chill, Jason pressed the shirt against her neck.

Over his shoulder, he saw Patron topple in a faint.

Yvette took that cue to join Jason's side. "Is she going to be okay? Her name is Leslie Cassel."

"Should be. Did she kidnap you?"

"Yes, but she's on my side. Interpol has been following Jacques for weeks. They needed the information in my brain to implicate him for taking bribes from a gunrunning operation moving through Lake Superior."

"Figured it was something like payouts," he said to Yvette. "Might have been his reason for sending you here. He had contacts in the area. Minnesota mafia."

"It makes too much sense now. And Interpol didn't call me in because they must have had no idea where to find me until recently. Jacques kept my location a secret."

She blew out a breath, and her body tilted against his. She was exhausted and probably didn't realize she'd leaned on him. Jason hugged her about the waist and bowed his head to hers. The moment was bittersweet, but he intended to remember only the sweetness of her body against his. "I couldn't pull the trigger, Jason."

"Because you're a good person, Amelie. Don't feel bad for that."

"But it's my job."

"It was your job. Now your job is to make sure Jacques Patron pays for his crimes."

"I can do that. I will do that. Now tell me how to help. Unless it involves getting half-naked?"

He chuckled and pulled on his coat and zipped it up. "That was a good shirt," he said. He switched positions with her, leaving her to triage. "Watch her. I'm going to take care of Patron."

He cuffed the man, who struggled, despite what had to be painful injuries.

"Got 'em," Jason said, feeling satisfaction for a job well done. "And without the CIA's interference."

They would assume control of the case from here. And take credit for it all.

Didn't matter. Jason had gotten to Amelie before Patron could harm her. He wished he could have found her sooner, so he could have protected

Leslie. This case had gotten him scrambling, and all had ended well.

With the suspect in hand.

"You saved me," she said from across the room. "I knew you would."

Jason caught her smile. It made the stormy day feel like springtime.

Epilogue

Days later…

Jason and Amelie stood beside the hospital bed where Leslie Cassel lay, recovering from the gunshot wounds. The damage had landed within centimeters of her artery, but fortune had not wanted her to die. She was eager to return to France and her job as soon as she could.

"I apologize for jumping the gun," she said to Amelie.

"I don't understand." Amelie moved closer while Jason clasped her hand. He'd taken to holding her hand lately. A lot. And she loved every single clasp.

"I won't apologize for kidnapping you. That was part of the job." Leslie smirked. "You know how we need to be covert for the integrity of an operation. But I should have waited. Lund was in jail…" She gave Jason a sharp glance.

Jason put up his hands. "I had no idea the guy was Interpol until a few hours before you took off with Yvette. Amelie." He gave her a wink. "I suspected he was another inept hit man. And really, for a trained agent, he should have known how to handle a snowmobile much better. I saved him from a plunge over a frozen falls."

"He told me that." Leslie smiled. Rutger Lund had been released immediately after Interpol had verified their agents had been sent to Frost Falls to extract the information from Amelie so they could make the case on Patron. He'd stopped in to visit Leslie before flying out of the country. "But I panicked. It was supposed to be a two-man operation. Pick up Amelie Desauliniers. Extract the information from her head. Send her to a safe house. We couldn't let you know we were from Interpol, Amelie, because we weren't sure if you were colluding with Patron."

"How did you finally decide I was not?"

"I didn't know for sure until the moment he faced you down in the repair shop."

"Nothing like coming down to the wire," Jason said. "Patron has been arrested."

"Yes, that's good," Leslie said. "But we never did get the information. And I'm sorry, Amelie, that things could have gone so wrong in that garage when Patron showed up. I thought I could handle it myself, but I needed backup."

"Apology accepted," Amelie said. "I know what it's like in the field and second-guessing your own judgment." She dug into her pocket and pulled out a piece of notebook paper to hand to Leslie. "Here's the list you wanted. But don't worry. I've already sent copies to the director at Interpol. Enough damning evidence to prove Jacques Patron was taking bribes from a gunrunner connected to the Minnesota mafia. And we've recovered the links from the original email, which lead to CCTV videos showing the handoffs in various major European cities."

Leslie folded the paper and closed her eyes. Pale winter sunlight beamed across her face. "Thank you. Are you going to be all right?"

Amelie nodded noncommittally. "I've already spoken to the director about the incident and have been debriefed. It's been suggested I remain in data tech, but I'm not so sure anymore."

"Don't let this scare you away," Leslie said. "You joined this organization for a purpose, yes?"

"I did. But that purpose may have been misdirected. It might have been more of a fearful reaction to a past event that made me follow in my father's footsteps. I'm going to give returning to Interpol some thought." Amelie looked to Jason, who squeezed her hand.

And Leslie also looked to Jason before smiling at Amelie. "I get it. This weather sucks. But the scenery..." She shook her head appreciatively. "I hear there's a calendar a girl should look at?"

"I think I know where to find you a copy," Amelie said. "We'll leave you to rest."

The twosome left as health services wheeled in a savory-smelling lunch. As they entered the chill outside air and walked toward Jason's truck, Amelie felt that what she'd told Leslie was the truth. She did need time to think about the job she'd always thought was the right fit for her. But it wasn't anymore. She had a misbalanced pros and cons list to prove that.

She'd been granted another week's leave before she was expected to report for duty. And she'd take it.

Jason opened the passenger door for her and helped her up inside his truck. Once seated, she reached for the door, but instead, Jason stepped up onto the side runner and leaned inside the cab to kiss her.

Even with the wind brisking her cheeks and bare hands with an icy chill, the heat they generated when their lips touched warmed her whole body. Amelie pulled him closer, and he leaned inside, reaching to embrace her about the waist as he deepened the kiss.

Leaving this man would be a challenge. But who said it had to happen right away? Or even… Dare she consider it?

When he broke the kiss, Jason bowed his forehead to hers, and for a while they simply shared the intense silence. Finally, he said, "Amelie. I love that name. I'll never forget that name."

Her heart did a flip-flop.

"I know you don't belong here," he said. "But maybe you could stay awhile longer?"

He wanted her to stay? Yes! "I do have a week leave. What if I extended my vacation here?"

"You'd do that?"

"I've been changed by my service with Interpol, Jason. I need to think of what it is I really want. Am I doing it because my parents were in it? Was it a fearful reaction to watching my mother get killed?"

He kissed her forehead. "Questions that only you can answer."

"What about you? Is the station still closing?"

"Probably. The CIA tossed me a freebie, though, and didn't step in on the case as I suspected they would. I got the credit for this one. And the sheriff's department called me this morning to offer me a position in Ely. I'm considering it."

"Is Ely another small town like this one?"

"A bit bigger." Seeing her frown, he added encouragingly, "They've got tourist attractions. And the wolf center."

"Wow. Exciting times abound here. But still cold, right?"

"Still cold." He leaned in, nuzzling a kiss at

the base of her ear, then whispered, "If you stay awhile longer, I'll keep you warm."

"That's an offer I won't refuse."

* * * * *

Get 4 FREE REWARDS!

We'll send you 2 FREE Books plus 2 FREE Mystery Gifts.

RANCHER'S HIGH-STAKES RESCUE
Beth Cornelison

KILLER SMILE
Marilyn Pappano

Harlequin® Romantic Suspense books feature heart-racing sensuality and the promise of a sweeping romance set against the backdrop of suspense.

FREE Value Over $20

YES! Please send me 2 FREE Harlequin® Romantic Suspense novels and my 2 FREE gifts (gifts are worth about $10 retail). After receiving them, if I don't wish to receive any more books, I can return the shipping statement marked "cancel." If I don't cancel, I will receive 4 brand-new novels every month and be billed just $4.99 per book in the U.S. or $5.74 per book in Canada. That's a savings of at least 12% off the cover price! It's quite a bargain! Shipping and handling is just 50¢ per book in the U.S. and 75¢ per book in Canada.* I understand that accepting the 2 free books and gifts places me under no obligation to buy anything. I can always return a shipment and cancel at any time. The free books and gifts are mine to keep no matter what I decide.

240/340 HDN GMYZ

Name (please print)

Address   Apt. #

City   State/Province   Zip/Postal Code

Mail to the Reader Service:
IN U.S.A.: P.O. Box 1341, Buffalo, NY 14240-8531
IN CANADA: P.O. Box 603, Fort Erie, Ontario L2A 5X3

Want to try 2 free books from another series? Call 1-800-873-8635 or visit www.ReaderService.com.

READERSERVICE.COM

Manage your account online!

- Review your order history
- Manage your payments
- Update your address

> ### We've designed the Reader Service website just for you.

Enjoy all the features!

- Discover new series available to you, and read excerpts from any series.
- Respond to mailings and special monthly offers.
- Browse the Bonus Bucks catalog and online-only exculsives.
- Share your feedback.

Visit us at:

ReaderService.com

RS16R